The
Mindtraveler

Bonnie Rozanski

Published by Bitingduck Press
ISBN 978-1-938463-39-6
© 2013 Bonnie Rozanski
All rights reserved
For information contact
Bitingduck Press, LLC
Montreal • Altadena
notifications@bitingduckpress.com
http://www.bitingduckpress.com
LCCN 2014920799

There is no difference between Time
and any of the three dimensions of Space,
except that our consciousness moves along it.

H. G. Wells, *The Time Machine*

CHAPTER 1

THERE WAS A LOUD rapping on my office door, before it was thrust open by a white-knuckled fist clutching a crumpled roll of paper. The fist, followed by the wide scarlet face and squat body of Caleb Winter, proceeded to shove the paper to within three inches of my face. Only three letters were visible on the curved surface: "NSF".

"What the hell is this?" he growled.

"Your laundry list?" I asked innocently. I knew exactly what it was, but I wasn't going to make it easy for him. Caleb might be the Department Chairman, but he's a misogynistic fool. We've had a long rocky history during the thirty years both of us have taught in Garriston U's Physics Department, Caleb coming the year after I did. That first meeting he attended, so cocky and full of himself—the one where he looked me up and down before directing me to go get him a cup of coffee: cream, no sugar—convinced me he was not worth listening to. And I'm pleased to say I never have.

Caleb waved the paper like a flag before my eyes. It was, of course, my latest grant proposal sent just yesterday to the National Science Foundation. As per Caleb's instructions, he has to be copied on every piece of correspondence.

"I've had about as much as I can take, Margaret. Your last proposal was bad enough—with all those loony ideas on how the future affects the past as much as the past affects the future. I mean, I gave you the benefit of the doubt, because, after all, physics doesn't actually rule out time going both ways. For particles, that is. But for people?" He laughed.

I didn't bother answering. It was a terrific idea that the NSF had rejected. No one thinks outside the box anymore.

Caleb slapped the proposal down onto the desk. As the paper unrolled its first line came into sight: "A Proposed Mechanism for Time Travel in the Macroworld, by Margaret Braverman."

"Do you honestly expect them to give you money for this?" he demanded.

Probably not, but I wouldn't tell him that. "Did you read it?" I asked, instead.

"As much as I care to."

"As I suspected," I said.

"A Mechanism for Time Travel" had already been thirty years in the making, involving deep meditation on the nature of space-time that I wouldn't expect Caleb to comprehend....

Of course, it has always been one of the curiosities of Maxwell's equations—the inspiration for Einstein's Special Relativity—that there are two different solutions for the calculation of an electromagnetic field. One describes a wave moving out from a particle into the future. The other describes an equal but opposite wave *from* the future back toward the particle. Physicists have always discarded the latter as being meaningless, like negative age or minus distance. But what if they were real—physical waves traveling back in time from the future?

"You're giving the Department a bad name," Caleb was saying. He must have given me a whole lecture, most of which I missed.

I looked up briefly as he glowered in my face. "All you want, Caleb, is the *status quo* —tiny little nano-increments of knowledge proving things we already know. *Someone* has to think big."

"That's your problem, Margaret. You're always coming up with these huge theories without any underlying foundation. If it weren't for the reputation of this department I wouldn't even mention it. Just let you send it in and deal with it yourself when it's rejected."

"I assure you that this time it won't be rejected," I replied with a certainty I didn't feel.

For a moment he looked flustered. "Who would be crazy enough to allocate money for this…?" All of a sudden, he gave me a knowing smirk. "…Not that old friend of yours we drummed out of academia and was lucky to score a spot at NSF?" Caleb grabbed the proposal back, leafed backwards to the last page, where he ran a stubby finger down to the bottom. "Ha!" he said, looking up. "cc: Frank Mermonstein."

"Leave Frank out of this," I cried out, surprising myself with my vehemence. "He was the only one in this godforsaken place who ever believed in me. I decided after Frank left to copy him on all my new work, and he could read it or not, just as he wished. For all I know, he may be throwing it in the trash can, but I've been sending it to him ever since."

"Right," Caleb said, dumping the packet back onto my desk and stalking out.

I sighed in the privacy of my office. Ah, Frank, lovely old Frank. I hadn't talked to him in years. Six foot one but so skinny the wind might have blown him away. Frank, who wore aviator glasses when everyone else was wearing wire rims, and corduroys when the whole world was wearing jeans, his hair short in the sixties, with sideburns in the eighties. Frank, who bucked all the trends. Frank, who never said a bad word about anybody, but got booted out, just as Caleb had said, when all he did was seek the truth. Ah, Frank. It was such a long time ago.

I glanced at my watch: almost three. Office hours were scheduled for one to three, but surely no one would be coming today. In fact, I couldn't remember the last time a student had shown up during my office hours. After thirty years of the same routine, I was tired, and I guessed it showed in my lectures. The last set of student evaluations had been pretty awful. "Phoning it in," I remember was one of the comments. "Doesn't seem to like students," said another.

I set aside the journal article I had been trying to read, got up and turned over the sign on my door from "Come in" to "Back tomorrow." I needed some air. And maybe I'd check in on my grad assistant at the lab. Not that Morgan needed much supervision; she was a real self-starter, probably more competent at setting up experiments than I was. My strength had never been hands-on anyway. My strength, if I have any, is Theory.

I took the stairs going down, because the tiny banged-up elevator in McArthur Hall was on the bum again, and at three o'clock, it didn't look like anyone would be by to fix it that day.

McArthur is one of the original buildings on campus. From the outside it has that old college feel, built of blocks of red brick with a host of architectural details: cupola, clock tower, and spires all dating back to the Thirties when the university was first founded. That's all well and good from the outside; it reinforces the traditional image of learned solemnity. But the inside is exactly what you'd expect in a structure eighty years old and largely neglected: stone steps worn concave by generations of adolescent feet; wooden railings polished to high luster by thousands upon thousands of soft young hands. A number of those adolescent legs raced past me now, with a wave and a smile, taking two steps at a time. As for my sexagenarian pair, they would have preferred the elevator, but going down three flights is better than going up. As for going back up, I figured I'd worry about that tomorrow.

The side door resisted but finally flung itself open when I put my whole body into it. Outside, the air felt fresh and warm for April, everywhere foliage unfurling with the energy and passion of youth. I exited the older part of campus, all collegiate brick and stone, and strolled past the Psychology Building, a long line of curved cement like some ungodly beached whale, built in the sixties when severe modern was all the rage. Then the Business building came into view, in the usual style of nineties steel and glass, and, beyond that loomed the new arena, a huge shiny monstrosity built in the early '00s when the university was flush with Wall Street alumni dollars. Ultimately, after generations of building the mode of the day, campus had become this riotous mosaic of styles, each building a mirror of the fashion and funds available at the time it was built, a history of the school as it ricocheted from Louis Kahn to Sarinaan to Frank Zwart and back again. A master plan there wasn't.

Students cut past me, impatient to get to wherever they were going; others clustered in the middle of the sidewalk, blocking foot traffic. Laughing, talking, shouting, dressed in high heels or flip-flops, tight skirts or baggy basketball shorts, black, white, tan, yellow, jabbering into their iPhones in English or Chinese or Spanish, they seemed as polyglot as the architecture.

On the far side of campus, I finally reached the science building, a late-seventies Carter-era marvel considered an architectural wonder at the time: hermetically sealed to retain the heat, with a shell of brushed steel and dark glass and windows that didn't open, its architects had apparently overlooked one thing—ventilation. It was sealed, all right.

I sometimes wonder whether someone was making an architectural statement on how we scientists seal ourselves off from the world…. Anyway, then there were four years of renovation with all the banging, the sawing, the dust and demolition. Thank God that's over.

Now, as I pulled at the heavy door, there was the sound of heavy suction, then all of a sudden, something like the pop of a vacuum-sealed can. Still sealed after all that effort. I crossed the marble antechamber to the bank of elevators and pushed seven.

As I entered the lab I could see Morgan, dainty brow puckered in concentration, straight black hair pulled behind her ears except for one lone strand dangling in her face, busy tweaking something in the wiring of our experimental set-up. On the work bench before her was arranged a Rube Goldberg array of equipment: lasers, prisms, splitters, fiber-optic cables.

Now for the past few years we'd been trying to prove the existence of a bizarre quantum feature called entanglement, and this would finally be the test. Entanglement, as I explain to my students, is the strange phenomenon in which two or more particles become so deeply linked that they share the same existence. Once photons—the fundamental units of light—have interacted, they can affect each other no matter how far apart in time or space they go. If you measure one, it has an immediate effect on the other no matter how far apart they are now.

Einstein called this "spooky action at a distance" and

called it impossible, because for it to happen, he said, the particles would have to be communicating instantaneously—in other words, faster than the speed of light. And that can't happen according to Relativity Theory. A paradox, yet….all the evidence supports it. So does Entanglement exist? That's what we're still trying to prove.

"Hi Dr. B," my assistant called out without looking up. Morgan Wong seems to know things without seeing them, something I can't quite explain but have no reason to complain about. She runs the whole lab—the equipment, the experiments, the subjects, all done smoothly, expertly, with geeky self-assuredness and American can-do spirit. She was brought up in Milwaukee, I think, despite the Asian surname.

Morgan came to me almost four years ago when she was still an undergraduate. She said she'd heard great things about my reputation and entreated me to be her thesis advisor. I never did find out who had said all those great things about me, but I was flattered, of course. After all, I wasn't exactly a household name. So I said yes, and that was probably the best decision I ever made. Morgan is a jewel.

On the table in front of her, a laser was poised to send its beam to a crystal, which would split each individual photon into two and send each on a different route. But the twin photons, coming as they have from a single beam, are what we call "entangled." If I measure them both at the end of the experiment, they should look exactly the same.

If they don't, physics as we know it may be wrong. Or, always a possibility, we just screwed up.

Morgan looked psyched. She put on her safety glasses and handed me mine.

I strapped on the glasses. "Okay, then."

"Cross your fingers," Morgan said before throwing the switch.

A brilliant beam shot out of the laser, split at the crystal and traversed the apparatus. The detector whirred into place. A digital camera clicked. The detector whirred again, and the camera clicked again, capturing whatever was on the detector's screen. Click, click, click, click.

"Okay, shut it off," I shouted, finally, over the noise of the equipment. "Let's see what happened."

As Morgan powered down the equipment, I sat down at the computer to pull up the results. The screen changed to show a series of graphs. The photon on the right, recorded on a detector that slid back and forth between two positions, showed alternating patterns: one of scattered dots, and one of light and dark rings. By all rights, this photon should force its twin to behave exactly the same. On the left, however, there was only a pattern of light and dark rings.

I shook my head in amazement, still staring at the screen. "I don't get it. The photons are entangled. The two patterns should be the same."

I took a look around for Morgan and noticed that she was back at the worktable with screwdriver in hand. I figured she was betting it to be a mechanical failure, since you can't fix Reality with a screwdriver. I'd just let her mess with the equipment awhile. Morgan would find the problem if anyone could.

Experimental misfires weren't unusual for me. Things mostly go wrong before they go right. What you need to do is not let the bad stuff stop you in your tracks. Fix it and try it again. And again and again. Make that finger in your eye prove itself to you before you give up. If you truly believe in something, do it—over and over, if necessary— because the next time it just might come out right.

I grew up on Long Island, a so-so girl in a so-so house on a so-so lot in a so-so town. My father worked in the City. My mother was a teacher. I thought my brother, two years older, got all the attention. Bill, apparently, felt that I did.

My parents worked hard at what they did, so that Bill and I wouldn't have to. They put us both through school, asking only that we get summer jobs. How they managed two Ivy League schools between us, plus law school for him and grad school for me, all told, fourteen years, all but two overlapping, I don't know. Young and stupid as we were, neither of us realized how good we had it then.

We had a dumb dog, Frisky. Part husky, part poodle, part lab, and part fish, she was forever jumping into the neighbor's swimming pool, but never able to haul herself out. At least six times a year, the neighbor called us on the phone to come rescue our dog. We tried asking Mr. Wilson to fence in the pool, but he told us instead we should lock up our dog. We tried confining her, securing all the doors so she couldn't get out of the house, but Frisky was an escape artist, materializing, Houdini-like, out of nowhere onto someone's lawn.

At one point, I tried to teach her how to climb a step-ladder, figuring that if she ever got herself into trouble she'd at least be able to generalize this behavior to the little ladder on the side of the pool. But, alas, no. One day she managed to get outside without anyone knowing it, on a day when the neighbor was away. When I came home from school—very late, because I stopped to gab with a buddy after chess club and then missed the last bus—the dog wasn't there at all. The most likely place, I figured, was that damned pool. I ran three houses down and there she was, floating belly-up in the water, black lips stiffened into a wide rictus that seemed to jeer, "Nyah, nyah, nyah. Got out of the house without your knowing."

We had a little ceremony and buried Frisky in the back yard, under the old peach tree. Bill played *Puff the Magic Dragon* on his guitar, as the rest of us took turns shoveling dirt on top of the corpse. She had a good life, we all said. She went the way she would have wanted to go. Of course, that was all bunk. We were just covering up our own sadness and guilt. Frisky never wanted to go at all. She never planned this to be her exit. It wasn't a suicide. That dumb dog just jumped into the pool as she always did, for the sheer joy of it, never considering, despite the dozens of times she tried that same stunt, that she'd never be able to pull herself out. You never know, she probably thought. The next time it just might come out right....

I was suddenly aware of Morgan pumping the screwdriver in triumph. "Faulty wiring," she exulted. "Back on line in a jiffy." What did I tell you?

"Okay," I said as we donned our safety glasses not long after. "Let's try this bugger again."

Morgan threw the switch. Again, a brilliant beam shot out of the laser, split at the crystal and traversed the apparatus to each detector. Whir. Click. Whir. Click.

I swiveled back to the computer screen. As before, one side showed that same pattern of dots, alternating with another of light and dark rings. This time, however, the other side showed those same two alternating patterns, back and forth, in tandem with its twin.

"Yes!" Morgan, looking over my shoulder, cried. "Entanglement exists!"

◊

By seven I was walking toward my Honda in the parking lot behind the science building. The wind had picked up, not unusual in Central New Jersey for April, and, though it had already turned dark, there was still plenty of light and activity. A stream of youngsters burst forth from the dining hall, laughing, from there budding off into smaller and smaller cohorts, some heading toward dormitories, others to night classes, concerts, or lectures. Lights glittered from the university center and the library; the arena beckoned with spotlights, and a lacework of street lamps crisscrossed the campus. Night or not, it was brighter than day.

I clicked the remote to open the car door, lowering my computer bag onto the passenger seat before sinking down behind the wheel. The experiment's success had lifted my spirits, but already I felt tired again. Did it matter what we discovered if I had no one to share it with?

I drove slowly through the dark windy streets for the two miles it took to reach my house, a small, dark green, Mission-style building; the kind they first put up in the Mission district of San Francisco but through some roundabout way ended up on a quiet street on the other side of the country. The house has thick masonry walls, arched windows with a low-pitched roof. The front door leads you right into the living room, as if to say, what you see is what you get. In fact, like me, my house has never tried to be anything but what it is. Inside is just the same as the outside: arched windows, plastered ceilings with exposed wooden beams. At one time I had been gung-ho about furnishing it with trestle tables and heavy wooden furniture, filling its decorative niches with ceramic pots, and covering four-poster beds with western-motif throws, but all that stopped twenty-five years ago. Or maybe it was twenty-four, I don't remember exactly; I stopped counting when I stopped caring. And I stopped caring, I guess, right after Frank left.

So now, as I entered the front door, everything was like

a time capsule from a quarter of a century ago—still the same arched windows and plastered ceilings with exposed wooden beams. Still the trestle tables, the ceramic *tchotchkas* in the decorative niches. But, a quarter of a century ago, I entered to a home filled with warmth and happiness; now all there was to greet me was a sad, dusty house.

I lowered my computer bag to the floor, hung up my coat in the hall closet, and slipped off my shoes. In my stockinged feet I traversed the long hallway that led to the kitchen, and opened the old built-in cabinet I kept the liquor in. The Jack Daniels was low; I had better replace it by tomorrow, I thought, because it wasn't going to hold out after tonight. I pulled out the bottle, got a glass from the cabinet over the microwave, threw in a few ice cubes from the freezer, and poured the contents in. Then I shuffled back into the living room, plunked myself down on the torn sofa and put my feet up on the old dented coffee table. And there I sat for the next two hours in a fog of memory and self-recrimination.

I could picture the first party I gave in this very living room. It was just after I'd bought the place, so it must have been sometime in '86 or '87. I had put twenty down on a mortgage of a hundred thousand—laughable really that this house ever cost a hundred and twenty thousand—but that was in the days just before the market spiked up and made it all but impossible, even in a backwater college town, for a professor to own her own home. My parents, God rest their souls, supplied fifteen of the twenty thousand for the down payment and told me to forget about paying it back. Of course, I protested that I couldn't possibly take it; they had scrimped and saved for most of their lives to put my brother and me through college, and they were sure to need it for themselves in the years ahead. But all they said was they had enough for the years ahead, thank you very much, and, anyway, what else would they do with it that could bring them greater happiness? So I took it. And it really did seem to bring them happiness. I'd have them over for a deli lunch or Dad would help me plant the garden—nothing too special, really, just some hours together away from the hot city streets. At any rate, it turned out that they didn't have so many years ahead.... Hard to believe I was older now than my mother was then, I reflected, taking a long slow slug of Jack Daniels.

Anyway, that was how I got the house. Once I had it, I decided that I wanted to give that housewarming party and to invite the whole department.

I stole a look at my watch, which informed me that it was way past dinnertime, maybe even time to stop drinking and go to bed, but all that accomplished was to get me to stand up, go back into the kitchen and upend the rest of the bottle into my glass. I rinsed out the bottle in the sink and stuck it in the blue box for recycling. Then I staggered back into the living room and picked up where I had left off.

It proved to be your usual university shindig: not a lot in the decoration department, but with a groaning table of good food and the island in the kitchen doubling as a makeshift bar. Naturally, there were people wandering all over the house; parking themselves in front of the bookshelf to browse my undergraduate copies of Bettelheim, Bertrand Russell or the collected plays of Ionesco. There were the typical polemics over string theory and Ronald Reagan, layered over the clink of ice cubes and the ripple of laughter, none of it in any way different from the drunken arguments at the annual Christmas parties at Dr. Joliet's, that stodgy old guy who was chairman of the Physics Department at the time. "Dr." Joliet, he insisted we call him, even though all the rest of us professors were on a first-name basis.

Hard to believe that Joliet himself has been dead for twenty years, I thought, taking another slug. I remember Frank made a pot of something. I can't say what, exactly. Maybe chili, because it was pungent and with such a fiery kick that all the guests kept doggedly at quenching the flame with a constant slosh of martinis, shaken not stirred, as I remember, by the self-appointed bartender, Caleb.

I lit the fireplace with some old alder logs I had found behind the house, but they were damp from the last rain and didn't catch right away. Frank wanted to help, offering me an unsolicited lesson on how you construct a teepee with kindling, but, of course, I had to do it myself, the end result being that we had as much smoke as heat for an hour or more. When the logs finally caught, though, it was with a heat so intense that the flame had a blue center.

Then, with only the small imposition of feeding logs to the beast I had created, the fireplace popped and crackled all night, scenting the room with the smell of a fir forest. It was glorious.

Of course, there was the incident where Caleb got drunk on his own martinis and made that sloppy, boorish pass at me; in the days when both of us were young and Caleb still thought of me as someone to make a pass at....I smiled ruefully into my drink.... And how Frank skillfully pulled him off me and walked him back to the living room to dose him with coffee. I never really thanked him for that, by the way. Or any of those other things. Any number of things I should have done but didn't.

I upended the glass to my lips, waiting for the last little legs of bourbon to dribble down the sides into my waiting mouth. Then I stood up as best I could and carried the glass off to the kitchen sink. Dinner seemed an afterthought by now, so I staggered upstairs to bed.

CHAPTER 2

THE EXPERIMENT ON ENTANGLEMENT had been just the first step in a series of quantum experiments. Quantum theory, FYI, describes the behavior of matter and energy at the atomic and subatomic levels, a level of reality underneath our own day-to-day one. In our world, for example, things must be here or there. In the quantum world, believe it or not, they can be here AND there. In our world, a cause precedes an effect; in the quantum world, effects may precede causes. QT even disagrees with both Newtonian physics and Einstein's theory of relativity. Let's face it, quantum theory is weird.

Quantum weirdness notwithstanding, the experiments we set up in the lab are fairly conventional. Caleb and the other physicists never called me a crackpot regarding any of those. Well, not that I know of, anyway. Of course, you can't tell what they're talking about behind your back when they go out for a beer or get together for fantasy football. But I'm an outcast just the same: one of two women in the department, and the only one really pushing the theoretical envelope. And there's the fact that twenty-five years ago, five years after I got here, I had that rather spectacular failure: a major embarrassment, where the only discernible result I got was setting my hair on fire. And no one's ever forgotten it, though no one talks about it aloud anymore.

Well, anyway, not that I know of.

Ever since, I've behaved myself in company. I've had my share of publications, all of them in particle physics, most of them in fairly respectable journals. But that's never been where my heart is. My heart is back with that quarter-of-a-century-old debacle. The holy grail of time travel.

Time travel: still a dirty word in physics. Even now, after the astrophysicist Kip Thorne has made wormholes respectable, when multiverses are all the rage, and black holes are in the news, my brand of time travel isn't acceptable. I send out proposals on the topic now and again. They've always been rejected, but I still have hope.

Meanwhile, I carry most of the experiment in my head—the equations, calculations, theoretical constructs. What is left I keep in the backroom of the lab. Morgan is the only one who knows anything about it, but Morgan is loyal to a fault, and I know I can depend on her to keep my secret....

◊

I WAS HEADED OUT OF the Science Building for lunch. Not quite able to face the noise and chaos of the Food Court today, I had the idea of getting in my car and going off campus, perhaps to Katz's Deli for one of their decadent corned beef sandwiches, though I knew what my cholesterol count would have to say about that. As I turned a corner toward the parking lot, however, I bumped right into the "Three Amigos"—Edwin Royce, Walter Maxwell and Mark Schwartz, longtime members of the Physics

Department who palled around socially.

Edwin, out in front as usual, short, wiry and pale, was a human dynamo idolized by his students, with a lifetime of protesting whatever presented itself. We used to joke Royce never met a cause he didn't like: gay rights; women's rights; acid rain; ozone hole growing larger; anti-war; anti-military; anti-Apartheid; blacks beaten in Georgia; Indians shot at in Wisconsin; prevent the CIA from recruiting on campus; oppose federal cutbacks in higher education. You name it, he fought it. Physics was just his sideline. Edwin's real occupation was protest.

Walter, though great friends with Edwin, was the complete opposite. If Edwin was the idealist, Walter was the pragmatist. If the ends were all-consuming to Edwin, then the means were the main point for Walter. What fascinated him were not the grand theories but the details of things, the inner workings. Not ambitious for himself, Walter was one of those people indispensable in working out the implications of other people's theories, replicating their experiments, and organizing a mountain of data. He preferred to retreat into the background, capable and diligent, but eclipsed by the brighter lights of Edwin and Frank. And maybe that was why I could never quite shake the picture of Walter, with his sharp features and small keen eyes, as a ferret sniffing around for roots and mushrooms in the forest.

Mark, finally, was our lone gay professor, his partner of thirty years having recently passed away of AIDS, despite the prodigious medical regimen of pills he was forced to take; the same regimen, by the way, that Mark had been taking ever since he had found he was HIV-positive. What these three guys had in common besides physics was beyond me, but where you found one, you'd inevitably find the others. Basically they were the only three in the department I could abide.

"Margaret!" Edwin cried, grabbing my elbow. "We're on our way to D'Amato's. Want to come?"

D'Amato's was the neighborhood pizza place, established in the thirties, if I remembered right, by Sal D'Amato, one of four brothers from Naples. Not long after, one of the other brothers started a competing pizzeria, and the whole family took sides—this one was lighter, that one was crispier, cheese on top or cheese on bottom; call it pizza or call it tomato pie. Each had its aficionados, its diehards. Me, I always patronized the Houston Street establishment: crisp thin crust, cheese on bottom, sauce on top, pure bliss.

I was surprised but tempted. I couldn't remember the last time I went out to lunch with the guys, but tomato pie sure sounded good. "Houston Street or Knowles Ave?" I asked, just to be sure.

"You can't be serious. Houston Street, of course," Mark said, making the required sour face at the thought of even considering patronizing enemy territory.

"All right then," I said. Knowles would have been a deal-breaker for me, too.

We all squeezed into Walter's SUV, because parking was always a problem in downtown Trenton, and headed for the old slummy part of the city, a backdrop of ruined factories and graffiti-covered brick faces, derelict old townhouses and broken-down bodegas, all set to an arrangement of Sinatra singing *Fly Me to the Moon* on Sirius radio in the background.

Across the street from a boarded-up warehouse and next door to a padlocked barber shop, its window saying, "Always open," hung a faded sign portraying an eternally steaming tomato pie. "D'Amato's," it proclaimed, as if it needed to. The parked cars were packed bumper to bumper all the way down the street, but around the corner, in a stroke of luck, a Land Rover was in the midst of pulling out. Walter eased us into the spot.

At ten to twelve there was already a line halfway down the block, of course. Waiting in line was one of the place's charms, along with no liquor license, no bathroom, and the surly attitude of the owner. D'Amato's had taken a whole host of off-putting negatives, every one of them making it quite clear how they didn't need you—how, in fact, they didn't even like you—and by the magic of complete indifference, made it to the top of Zagat's *Not to be missed* list.

By twelve-thirty we were in and ensconced, not so comfortably, in one of the ancient Naugahyde, one-size-fits-all booths. The table was a thin veneer of fatigued Formica, the swirl of its fifties' pattern worn off in the center to a bare white blur. Frank Sinatra and Frankie Valli posing with a skinny young Sal; Anthony Scalia and Samuel Alito shaking hands with a fatter, older one, all smiled out from mismatched frames atop distressed knotty pine paneled walls. Zagat reviews marched along the walls, decade by decade extolling the brilliance of the tomato pies.

Be it ever so humble, there's no place like D'Amato's. From where we sat, I could just make out the TV positioned high in the corner of the room, up where the wall meets the ceiling, and tuned silently as always to the Philadelphia Phillies. From the look of it, they were losing to Atlanta, but it was hard to tell with no sound. Around us sat twenty tables of ecstatic customers waiting stoically for their pies in the clattering cold of the lone air conditioner, lifting their eyes now and again to watch Jimmy Rollins or Carlos Ruiz at bat, laughing and guzzling their BYO beer, above all smugly pleased with themselves for having beaten out the other twenty-five people still sweating outside on line in the heat.

Meanwhile, Edwin had been on his iPhone the entire time, coordinating some nationwide teach-in for something or other. "I'll be finished in a minute," he said for the tenth time, keying something in with a lightning-fast thumb. He briefly looked up from his text. "I really hope you guys will show up next Tuesday for the Occupy Movement teach-in."

I must have been rolling my eyes, because Edwin turned on me. "Honestly, Margaret. We're on the side of the angels here. What part of the Occupy agenda can you possibly object to?"

I thought for a moment before answering. "Do they actually have an agenda?"

Edwin punched one last button before gently placing the iPhone to the left of the salt shaker. "Do we have an agenda? How about overwhelming corporatization of the nation, greed of the Wall Street bankers, immorality of past and present politicians, the decline of education and health…?"

"In other words, everything," I interrupted, smiling.

"Hey, it's all broken," Edwin shot back. "You realize that the top 20% of Americans own 85% of the country's wealth and the bottom 80% of the population owns 15%? That the top 1% of income earners nearly tripled their after-tax income over the last thirty years, while the rest of us 99% dropped 36.1%?"

"Calm down, Edwin," Mark told him. "We're not the enemy."

"No, but we're all in it together. We are the 99%!" Edwin proclaimed, fist in the air. It sometimes seemed to me that Edwin's fist had been in the air for the past thirty years. And what had he accomplished? What had any of us accomplished?

A young man in a backwards baseball cap leaned across the aisle to ask, "When and where's the protest, Dude?"

"Tuesday, 11:00 in front of the Garriston Administrative Building," Edwin answered. "We'd be happy to have you."

"Thanks, we'll be there," the guy said, leaning back.

"See?" Edwin said to me. "Young people see the value of protest."

"You're right, Edwin," I replied. "I guess I'm just an old fart." No one contradicted me.

"Hey, I actually think she's coming over to take our order," Mark was whispering, tracking Angela D'Amato, the owner, with his eyes as she approached, then passed us without a glance. "No, I guess not."

We watched as the four guys across the aisle got two tomato pies. One pan was dumped unceremoniously onto the Formica, the other thrown Frisbee-like to rest on top and slightly overlapping the first, the bottom one difficult to get at now, and the two of them taking up four-fifths of the tabletop. On principle, D'Amato's eschewed any high-tech doodad like stacking racks that might save space.

"Hot!" said one of the table mates, grabbing a slice and dropping it back down before he risked another try, finally taking a big bite.

D'Amato's thin-crust pies, by the nature of the beast, started off blazing hot, but within five minutes were cold and hard as a rock. You learned to eat fast.

"Hot!" the guy said again, this time through his teeth, then a few open-mouthed pants, before "Mmmmm."

He caught my eye, and I realized I had been staring. "Good?" I asked.

He nodded and my mouth watered. With reluctance, I tore my eyes away from his slice.

"What'll youse have?" I heard all of a sudden. Angela

D'Amato was standing in front of us with her usual expression of disdain, a notepad in her hand.

"Pepperoni? Banana peppers? Garlic? Clams?" Mark asked us.

"Sounds good," said Edwin, still peering down at his iPhone.

"Which?" Mark asked.

Edwin said nothing, lost in a text.

"Say, pepperoni and banana peppers on one, garlic and clams on the other," Walter said. "That all right with you, Margaret?"

"Sounds good," I said.

Angela wrote something down with a flourish and turned on her heels.

"That'll be another twenty minutes, at least," Mark said sadly, looking at his watch.

We sat there a few moments with nothing much to say. Finally I turned to Mark. "How are you?" I asked.

He gave me a sweet, bitter smile. It was hard to read Mark. On the one hand he was looking good. That is, aside from a hump at the back of his neck, the after-effect of that cocktail of drugs he had to take to save his life but which coincidentally removed fat from places like his cheeks which, now that I looked at them, seemed strangely gaunt. And then the fat transmogrified into that curious hump, which, again, now that I looked at it closely, made him look a little like a camel. Aside from those things, he was looking good.

On the other hand, I couldn't tell what was going on inside, now that his partner Jerry was gone. And so quickly, too. I wasn't sure I had ever heard the full story, but if Mark didn't want to tell me, I wasn't going to push him.

"Not bad," he said, looking off into the distance in the direction of Angela's back.

Another few moments of silence. "How are your classes?" I asked.

That same sweet, bitter smile. Rumor had it that Jerry finally, in a fit of despair, drowned himself in the bathtub after drinking a vast amount of Jameson's whiskey. Wrote a long note of apology detailing the reasons why, and that Mark would surely find someone else more worthy. Something like that. Bits and pieces of the incident floated around from a number of reliable and unreliable sources. Probably not the full story, but expecting Mark to spit it all out had about the same probability as winning the Pennsylvania lottery.

"Fine. Good," Mark answered. "Had a great crop of students this year."

I considered trying to draw him out one more time, but if he wasn't going to tell me anything juicy, what really was the point?

Another few moments of silence, punctuated by laughter and chewing noises from the other tables. A tall blond boy in a tomato-splotched apron came by to bring a set-up of napkins, cutlery, and the same green Melmac dishes they've used since the fifties. We gave in our drink order: two waters, a Coke and a Seven-Up.

"So," Walter said all of a sudden. "I've decided to retire next year."

There was a collective gasp. Walter was the *éminence grise* of the Garriston Physics Department, that powerful decision-maker who operates behind the scenes; the unofficial Chair; the guy who organized things when Caleb was too lazy or too drunk to do it himself. Walter was there when I came, and somehow I expected he'd be there forever. So, I guess, did everyone else.

"You don't have to, you know," Edwin said, lifting his eyes from the little screen. "The Federal Age Discrimination in Employment Act of 1994 abolished mandatory retirement for tenured professors at age seventy. The university can't force you to retire or reduce your status. Other than denying you a raise or making your life miserable in one way or another—and I suppose Caleb would be happy to find a way—they can't do much to make you retire without violating federal law. Me, I plan to work forever."

Ugh, I thought. Who would actually want to work forever? Or live forever, for that matter?

"You think I don't know that, Edwin?" Walter said. "Don't worry about me. I've got it all worked out. The dean and I worked out a great deal. He's offering me 80% of my salary for two years if I leave by next June. That's 80% of $112,000 x 2…"

"$179,200 total," Mark contributed.

"…Yeah, plus, I've accumulated $1,400,000 in my pension plan, and I'll get 4% of that annually."

"$56,000 a year," I added, just to get into the conversation.

"Right," Walter said. So, I've got $145,600 per year for the first two years, and $56,000 per year after that, added to my Social Security, not to mention what I've made in the market. I'm good."

"If the market doesn't tank," Edwin said.

"Believe me, the market's on its way up to 20,000," Walter replied.

"You wish," I said.

"Anyway, I worked out this terrific deal with the dean: an office; I'm permitted to teach one course per semester; do research in my lab. If I continue to do grants, I get a grad student. That, on top of emeritus status, and a paid-up membership in the University Country Club. I got the dean to sign off on everything."

"I don't know how much they offered you, but I'm sure you could get a lot more," Edwin said, putting his phone down. "The administration is holding out on you. If you rejected the offer, they'd offer more."

"It's enough," Walter said. "The money's worked out."

We sat in silence for a few minutes, amid the clatter of dishes and a cacophony of table talk.

"You really want to retire, Walter?" Mark asked, finally.

Walter blinked. From his demeanor I wondered whether he'd ever actually confronted that question. "Well, I've been here forty-five years," he said at last. You think I plan to work forever?"

"*Do* you?" I asked.

"Why not?" Edwin said.

Walter said nothing. With all his financial planning, I had the feeling he didn't have a clue as to what he was getting into.

"You got any hobbies?" Mark asked.

Another blink. "I'll get some. Golf, maybe."

The three of us snickered at the thought of Walter on a golf course. All he'd ever done as far as we knew was to work in his lab.

"And Eileen," I volunteered. "What does she think of your retiring?"

Walter cleared his throat for several seconds. "My wife says now she'll have me at home twice the time at half the pay."

Edwin laughed.

"Uh oh," Mark said.

"Walter, don't do this," I implored, suddenly worried for him.

"Figure it this way," Mark said, trying a different tack. "If you work ten more years at $112,000 a year—discount that at 8% a year because it's future dollars—so that's $103,040 a year. Ten times that is $1,030,400. So, if you work ten more years, you get over a million dollars as opposed to $179,200 all inclusive for the first two years and $56,000 a year for the next eight, which comes to," he paused for a microsecond, "$627,200...."

"Yeah, for a total deficit of $403,200," Walter interjected. "I know, Mark. You think I haven't done the math? I'm good. I've got enough."

"Okay, then," Mark said. "I'm just trying to consider your welfare."

"Thank you, Mark. I appreciate that."

"Besides," Walter said after a pause. "After forty-five years of teaching, I'm tired." He trained his beady eyes on me for some reason, and suddenly that ferret face of his looked every one of his sixty-nine years. "Aren't you ever tired, Margaret?" he said.

I considered the question to be rhetorical, and besides the young man with the tomato splotched apron had just appeared with the pies, so I never did answer Walter's question. But it got me thinking. Boy, was I tired.

The waiter dropped the garlic and clam onto the Formica, and slid the pepperoni and banana pepper at an angle on top. "Enjoy," he said and headed back to the oven.

We chewed awhile.

"You really going to play golf all day?" I couldn't help but ask.

Walter just kept chewing.

"We'll miss you," Mark said.

"Don't worry," Walter told him. "You won't get rid of me that easy."

That was pretty much the conversation. The whole retirement dialectic had kind of killed the mood, I guess. We finished all the pies with relish but not with a lot of added talk. When we were done, we each chipped in ten dollars, and I brought the haul over to their antique cash register, where Angela rang it up without a word. Of course, it wouldn't have cost her anything to say, "Thanks for coming," but it just wasn't her style. And no need, after all. Zagat rated the place thirty-four for food, but only two for décor, and still, we schnooks kept coming in droves. Who needed to be nice?

The four of us walked back around the block to Walter's SUV, hoisted ourselves in and made our way back to campus, past the ruined factories and graffiti-covered brick faces, past the derelict old townhouses and broken-down bodegas, all set this time to Peggy Lee on Sirius radio crooning *Is That All there is?*

CHAPTER 3

IT WAS EARLY MAY, exam time for the undergraduates, as I entered the lab. The set-up on the worktable looked almost the same as it did a month and a half ago. A laser aimed its beam to a crystal, and from there, the twin photons in each split beam took different paths.

There was but one change. Morgan, at my direction, had wired up the right side through several miles of coiled-up fiber-optic cable, delaying the photons by what we expected would be about fifty microseconds. Because of the delay, the beam would arrive at the detector on the left fifty microseconds before the photon on the right. That was the only difference.

But its implications were great. Remember, the photon on the right, recorded as it was on a detector which slid back and forth between two positions, was the one which "decided" which pattern to show. But the photon on the left, entangled as it was with its twin, would display the result of that decision before it had ever been made.

Morgan seemed to be in an uncharacteristic tizzy. As I entered she was staring out one of the hermetically sealed windows, watching so intently that she didn't even hear me come in.

When I said, "hello," she jumped. Her mouth smiled at me, but the lips were twitching.

"What?" I asked.

She shrugged.

"You and your boyfriend fight again?" For the four years I had known Morgan, she and her boyfriend Kenny were on again/off again/on again/off again. Clearly it was a love/hate relationship, more love than hate or it wouldn't have lasted four years, but I could never keep track of whether they were on or off. From the look of it today, they were off.

"No. We're good," she said.

I looked Morgan squarely in the eye, but all I got out of it was another twitchy smile. "So what is it, then?" I asked.

A long pause. "I kind of hope it doesn't work," she confessed finally, nodding at the set-up.

"The experiment?" I asked, incredulous.

"Just the implications, I guess," she replied, looking out the window again. "It kind of offends me to think that the future should be able to affect us in the present."

Retrocausality, or reverse causality, where an effect occurs before its cause, was what this experiment was meant to demonstrate, at least in principle. Einstein never liked the idea either.

"But you've been working up to this for three and a half years," I said.

"I know," she agreed, turning her head back to look at me. "Silly, isn't it?"

"Maybe not so silly," I replied, not committing myself either way. I understood the desire for a young girl to make her own mistakes, but I'm old enough now to wish I could just go back and erase them.

Morgan was back to looking out the window, winding and unwinding one lone strand of hair onto the index finger of her right hand. I wondered what she was looking for out there. "I'd like to feel I'm free to live my life any way I choose," she said in a whisper.

Why did I have the feeling that her Chinese Tiger mother might be the real reason behind this, not the arrow of time? I'd heard stories about her once upon a time: how she made Morgan practice the piano for three hours a day, even on vacation; how A- was a bad grade and a silver medal a piece of garbage.

I walked up behind Morgan, placing a maternal hand on her shoulder, and we stared out the window together for a bit. The sky was a vivid blue with an assortment of fluffy clouds, some tiny ducks floating on a far-off pond.

"Kenny wants us to get married," Morgan said, out of nowhere.

So this was what was really bothering her. "But you don't?" I asked.

She sighed. "Kenny says I can't commit."

"Maybe it's that you just can't commit to *him*?"

"No. I really love Kenny," Morgan retorted. She turned toward me, trading a long earnest look for my skeptical one.

We stood looking out the window for a few minutes. All the usual droves of kids were crisscrossing campus on their way to class. Two young men in shirtsleeves were busy sailing a Frisbee back and forth across the quad. Whatever the strange laws of time and space, life went on its merry way.

"You know my parents are divorced," she said.

"No, I didn't."

"It was bad," she said to the window. "Really bad. My father had an affair, and my mother threw him out of the house, screaming like a banshee, throwing his clothes onto the sidewalk. I was very young, but the scene is like tattooed into my brain. And she never forgave him, not even a little bit. For the next twenty years it was how much she hated him, how men are garbage, how they're only out to get into your pants." Morgan shivered with the memory. "The whole idea of marriage makes me panic. I guess that's why I can't commit."

We stood another minute at the window, the sky darkening into dusk.

"You know, not committing has the often unintended effect of ending up alone," I said. "That may be fine at 24, but at 60, not so much. Don't let your emotions make your decisions for you."

She must have picked up on the point that I had done that very thing. "Why should you regret not marrying?" Morgan asked, turning toward me. "You're a successful scientist."

I doubted whether I was really the success in science Morgan seemed to think I was. Even if I were, it was at a cost. "What I wouldn't give to go back and do things differently," I said.

Morgan looked at me strangely. "Maybe you should."

I briefly wondered what she meant by that, then decided I didn't want to know. "Well," I said, instead. "I don't think we solved your problem with life, but I don't really think it's about the retrocausality. And if it is, let's face it, this experiment may not even work. But we won't know till we do it, so why don't we get started?"

Morgan laughed, back to her normal unflappable self. "Okay, let's do this."

We shut off the lights, and Morgan threw the switch. As before, a brilliant beam shot out of the laser, split at the crystal and traversed the apparatus. Patterns of light and dark rings lit up the left detector screen.

As the detector whirred into place but before the camera had time to click, the ring pattern on the left detector dissolved into one of scattered dots. But then it was back to the ring pattern again. The whole thing was so quick, it was hard to figure out what had really happened.

I sat down at the computer and pulled up the experimental results, which confirmed that the dot pattern on the left detector appeared exactly fifty microseconds before the right detector could ever have made the selection. And there it was—the effect before the cause.

"Shit," said Morgan.

◊

I'M ALL FOR REPLICATING results that you don't agree with, but if the universe is telling you something, you really have to listen. If, on some fundamental level, effects can precede causes, then we just have to accept it and move on. In the end, what's true is true. You can't just bend the universe around to your personal liking.

I guess I've always been a geek. In high school I'd regularly tell the teachers what they were doing wrong. Like the time in Chemistry where Mr. Hudson, who was a Fundamentalist Christian if I remember right, went way off on some tangent about how the orderliness we see in the universe—solar systems; evolution; mankind, you name it—proved that there was a God. Entropy, the tendency of a system to disorder, he said, meant that everything winds down instead of up. For instance, a glass that falls off a table and breaks into a zillion pieces is a common event, but the chance that it would fall upward from the floor and reassemble itself on the table is pretty near impossible. So, Mr. Hudson concluded, without a God to wind it back up again, the universe would be a cold soup.

This lunacy just got on my nerves. Without even raising my hand I lectured him on how there can be subsets of increasing order even if the larger whole tends toward disorder. I seem to remember giving examples, as he turned red, and the class tittered. Mr. Hudson conceded that point to me but said it didn't apply to this situation. Then he went back to diagramming molecules or whatever he had been doing before he made the mistake of going off topic. He didn't look in my direction again for the rest of the semester.

I'd do this stuff again and again, damn the consequences. I'd beat a guy at tennis just to show I could, despite the fact that that very guy was the one I desperately wanted to invite me to the prom. Needless to say, Spencer never asked me. I ended up going with a fellow geek from the chess club. I still have a photo of the two of us: me, five foot ten in sky blue chiffon and size nine matching pumps, and Shelly, his head just reaching to my shoulder, in what looks like his Bar Mitzvah suit.

◊

I LET MORGAN LEAVE EARLY. She had a paper due and she needed time to work all this out, anyway. As soon as the door closed, I unlocked the backroom and went in. The room has no windows. It isn't a lot bigger than a storage closet, and sometimes does double duty as one. But it has access to expensive electronics and as much electricity as I require. And it's a place with some vivid memories. It's where I set my hair on fire.

Thirty years I've been in this lab. It's the first and only lab I've had at Garriston, and short of graduate school on the West Coast, I've never done research anywhere else. While the front room is witness to the conventional stuff, the backroom is for the crazier, off-the-wall, mad-scientist theories, and the experiments to prove them. It's for the hits or misses, the trials and errors, the crack-pot dreams, all the things I don't want the world to know about until they prove me right. The room doesn't judge me or call me names. It can't tell right from wrong except to show me what works and what doesn't. Morgan knows about it but has never been inside. There is only one key, and that's on my keychain.

I locked the door from the inside before I turned on the overhead lights. In the corner was the sort of chair you might find in a barber shop or a hair salon, with a large helmet-like dome perched on a sliding vertical pole, much like one of those hair dryers that the stylist might pull down over your newly set head....or do they even do that anymore?

But looking closer, one could distinguish at least a few differences in the helmet. Inside, for instance, there is no heat source. Instead, there is a blanket of electronic sensors, each connected to the helmet by a myriad of wires. And the whole contraption is enclosed in a heavy lead shield. Further, if you look around the room, you might find similar, smaller prototypes with trays underneath on which an object might rest; others with clamps added for holding specimens that might not sit still.

Like my house, it's all been here for thirty years, but unlike my house, there's not a speck of dust anywhere. It may not look like it, but it has been a working laboratory all this time engaged in proving that if the body can't travel in time, perhaps the mind, emerging like a magnetic field out of the electric labyrinth of the brain, can.

Just as our Everyday world emerges from the quantum world with its own laws and postulates, the mind has an independent existence with its own rules. Frank was the only other faculty member in the department who was open-minded enough to talk about it. The others were horrified.

I sent off a proposal to the NSF with the title of "Time Travel of an Entangled Mind" and never even got a response. Meanwhile, proud of myself, I sent a cc: to Dr. Joliet. I will never forget the department meeting that followed.

"Margaret," Dr. Joliet, a white-haired gentleman even then, gentle and courtly to me unless provoked, began with quiet concern. "Are you well?" he asked me.

When I assured him I was quite well, thank you, he couldn't contain himself any longer.

"Out of the box thinking is all very well, my dear, but this is insanity," he boomed from the head of the conference table. "Our department is not psycho-physics; it's physics. And, yes, quantum theory is weird as they say, but it has very accurate mathematics that predicts all sorts of proven phenomena. How can you even attempt to prove this... this...mystical mumbo-jumbo?" His normally kindly face was contorted and red.

Then there was a cacophony of voices, most with something damning to say. Caleb called me some name, I don't remember what. Walter wanted to reevaluate my tenure track. Frank, though he made an eloquent case for not rejecting what we don't yet understand, got shouted down, as did Dr. Joliet. Only Henri D'Amboise, with his deep Caribbean-flavored *basso profundo*, was able to cut through the din and bring everyone to order.

By the end of the meeting, I was left with one over-whelming message. If I were to continue on as a valued member of the Garriston University Physics Department; if I were ever to aspire to tenure, I, Margaret Braverman, should cease and desist in this ridiculous New Age specu-lation and return to the fold of responsible physics. By all means, Dr. Joliet allowed, investigate quantum theory, en-tanglement, and even time if you must, but never mention time travel in body or mind again.

I kept to my end of the bargain for several years. I never mentioned it again, except to Frank. And all of my exper-iments for public consumption were conventional enough and within the fold enough that I was awarded tenure three years later. But behind the locked door of the storage closet I did my real research.

There are some who say that consciousness is inherent in all matter, that it is the total information in the whole, above and beyond the relationships between its parts. That the higher the value, the more conscious the thing. By that reckoning, of course, even a rock might have a kind of consciousness.

I mean, a rock doesn't seem to be doing much of any-thing, but at the micro-level, it's this huge number of atoms connected together, all bouncing around in response to the gravitational and electromagnetic signals it detects in the universe. What if the atoms in this rock vibrate in a way that somehow creates a sentient mind? Even if it only thinks one thought every million years, that rock is conscious.

So, open-minded as I am, I first built small prototypes with trays underneath and tried to send simple inanimate objects nanoseconds into the future. Unfortunately, whatever micro-jump I could achieve was so tiny an interval that it was all but impossible to see if the object had actually gone anyplace. It just sat there…like a rock. Perhaps, I thought, a rock is just a rock, after all.

Therefore, I proceeded on to small animate objects—first lizards, then mice. Some of the lizards didn't make it. I had more success with the mice, presumably because they have more awareness. And it worked! Oh, not for long. First it was only for microseconds, then milliseconds, and finally after many tries, long enough to see the mouse slump down into a stupor before in a flash it was back again, eyes open and alert. None of them seemed to be worse for wear, but of course, there was always the question of whether the animal was truly transported in time or whether it was merely anesthetized. I wanted to use bigger animals, on the assumption that there would be more of a conscious mind to send, and then more of a mind to test, but by then the animal rights fanatics on campus had made it impossible to even secure a bigger animal on which to experiment. Finally, having exhausted small reptiles and mammals, and needing to ascertain where their consciousness had gone, there was nothing left to experiment on…but myself.

So, twenty-five years ago today at 5:03 in the evening,

with Frank as my reluctant accomplice, I was sitting in this very chair. We were operating on the assumption that after twenty-five years I would still possess the helmet and would remember to put it on at the right time, because for this to work, there needed to be both a sender and a receiver. That was the only way to insure that we would have a receiver in a comparable helmet at the set time. Thus, we established a window in time, from May 3, 1987 at 5:03 p.m., to May 3, 2012 at 5:03 p.m., in which my younger self would transport herself to my body.

Needless to say, something went wrong, and I would have electrocuted myself if Frank hadn't been there to kill the power. I've pondered why this happened, finally coming to the conclusion that it could only have been at the sending end. A small short allowed the power to enter my head *from* the electrodes instead of sending it from my head *into* the electrodes. Of course, I've long since fixed the problem, but the window in time had closed. Frank had moved on; there was no one else I could truly trust, and I feared going it alone. I continued to transport mice from milliseconds to seconds to hours to days in the future. The mice would slump down, senseless, until, moments later they would suddenly rouse themselves and look around. There was no reason why it couldn't be years, if I chose.

I thought of it now and then, but had long since given up the idea of using it on myself again. Going into the future would put me in an even older body, and one which, for all I knew, wouldn't be around when I expected it to be.

But somehow this discussion with Morgan had fired me up again. It was May 3. The time, according to my watch, was 4:48 in the afternoon. Why not? I asked myself. I had just proved that time goes in reverse. I could go backwards instead of forwards, if I chose. My younger self was sure to be ensconced in the contraption by five p.m. There was no uncertainty about that. If I initiated the process at five, I would be the sender, and she the receiver. Should I?

I lovingly fingered the helmet. Should I? I had no accomplice this time to pull me out in the event that something went wrong. It could strand me in some time-less limbo where I might float forever. And I hadn't told anyone about this. If I were gone, would they even know how to get me back? I glanced again at my watch: 4:56. The window was closing. The clock was ticking. It was now or never.

I set the instrument panel to the required parameters, sat down on the chair and pulled the helmet down over my head. I stretched my right arm as far as I could to reach the small black button on the back side of the helmet and placed my finger lightly on top. The dial of my watch, facing toward me, said 4:59. The moment it turned five, I pressed the button.

That very instant, I lost all touch with my body. All that I was seemed to be disembodied consciousness. There was no sensation of space or of time or of anything, for that matter. No noise, but no silence. No light, but no dark. No something, but no nothing. Me was all there was.

Thinking, therefore I was. Until suddenly I could see again, feel again. Frank was at my side, exactly as I remember him, in his side burns and aviator glasses, staring into my eyes with great concern.

"Get me out of here!" I tried to shout, but my mouth wouldn't work. My hands seemed to belong to someone else. My watch, an entirely different watch from the one I had had on a split second ago: the one with a leather band and the small white watch face with golden numerals that my parents had given me for graduation—said 5:01.

"Abort! Abort!" I screamed, but no words came out. If I didn't get out of here, I'd have to go through that horrific shock I remembered all too well: ten milliamps of electricity shooting through my body, setting my hair on fire. 5:02: all I could do was to wiggle my right pinky finger on the armrest in the chair.

"What's the matter?" Frank asked, staring at the wayward pinky. He peered through the eyeholes of the helmet, startling at the terror in my eyes. "Do you want to abort?"

"Yes! Yes! Abort!" I tried to shout, but the mouth said, "Of course not."

Frank backed up, looking confused. "Then why are you…"

All of a sudden, 5:03 clicked into being and I went through the most hellish experience of my life—AGAIN. Electricity coursed through my head, my body convulsing for what felt like forever until Frank reached behind the contraption and pulled the plug out. I slumped over like a discarded marionette, my hair on fire, as Frank threw himself on top of me to extinguish the flames, sealing his lips to mine in four long breaths of life.

There was something so familiar, so delicious, in Frank's body bearing down on me, his lips pressed hard against my own. I had almost forgotten the sensation.

"Oh, my God, Margaret. I thought I'd lost you," he said, as my eyes finally opened. "Are you okay?"

My hair, a moment ago thick and honey blonde, was now sooty wisps of charcoal. My clothes were scorched and smoking. The leather of my watchband had evaporated, leaving a tattooed replica where it used to be. Altogether, I felt exactly as one would feel who has just come back from the dead: exhausted, hurting, exhilarated, and very much alive. I wanted to shout, "Yes, yes! I'm wonderful!"

The words that came out of my mouth, instead, were, "What the hell did we do wrong?"

"I don't know yet," Frank said, lifting me to my feet. "But you seemed to have some foreboding before it happened. I could see it in your eyes."

"Foreboding?"

"Yes. And you were wiggling your little finger."

"I don't know what you're talking about." My body, scorched and smoking, but twenty-five years younger and twenty pounds lighter than I remembered being just a moment ago, stepped away from Frank and brushed itself off.

I say this because that is exactly the way it seemed to me.

I could feel myself moving and talking, but I had almost no control over it. Though I could hear no one's thoughts but my own, it was clear that my other self was not only still there, but had dominion over our one sole body. In fact, it was plain that I- the older me—was the trespasser, about as useful as an extra head on a single body; my host had no idea I was even there. All I could do was tag along and passively witness everything that I had witnessed before. I'd been there and done that. What was the point of going back in time if you could do nothing to change it?

"Maybe we should take you to the university hospital," Frank said, examining the smoking ruins of me. "You've had a nasty shock."

"No way," I said. "Do you think I'm actually going to publicize what happened here?"

That is, that is what came out of my mouth. At this point, I'm going to have to dispense with who it was who actually said what. Clearly, the mouth was of Margaret, aged 35, along with the tongue, teeth and the rest of the body. I—Margaret, aged 60—could sense and feel, even thrill in the easy movement of thirty-something toned limbs, but until I figured out how to influence things, 60 was just along for the ride.

"You sure you're okay?" Frank asked again, bringing over a hand mirror.

The image gave me—both of me—quite a shock. The hair in the mirror was frizzled, the eyebrows singed. But it didn't faze 35, who laughed. "Yes, yes. I'm fine. I've just got to figure out what to do with my hair."

My raincoat, I knew, was hanging on the coat rack near the outer door. Though my mind was slightly hazy, I seemed to remember a kerchief I'd jammed in the pocket. My alter ego clearly remembered these things as well. I stood up to open the door to the outer lab but suddenly found myself—or rather, Frank found me—passed out on the floor. As I came to, he was cradling my head in his lap.

"What happened?" I asked him.

"You're not okay," he told me definitively. "I'm taking you to the hospital."

"No, no! You can't! Then everyone will know what happened!"

"Margaret, you have to be checked over," Frank told me, pulling me back up to the barber chair. "There could be internal bleeding, even neurological damage."

I wanted to tell him that I had gone through this whole thing before; the doctors had checked me up, down and sideways, and they had never found anything. But the whole issue was moot, because my mouth said, "I won't go."

"You're being irresponsible," he replied.

"No, I'm being very responsible," I countered. "I've got tenure. They can't fire me. But if anyone finds out that you were assisting me, your head will be on the chopping block." Then, while Frank stopped to digest this, I added, "Think of your wife and baby girl, for heaven's sake."

"You're right about that," he said after a pause. "I've got to think about them first. But you really need to go to the hospital."

I don't, I tried to say, but that went nowhere, of course. I was like a newborn baby. I could feel my torso, arms, legs, and tongue, but I couldn't figure out how to make any of it work.

"Tell you what," my mouth said. "I'll go if you agree to leave me at the front door of the hospital. Then leave. Burn rubber and drive off. So, help me God, Frank, I don't want you involved at all."

"Deal," Frank said, already helping me off the chair. I had the feeling he had already figured out the situation way before me, the way he'd play chess—sixteen moves ahead of his opponent. Frank was a good-looking guy in a lean and hungry Willem Dafoe sort of way, but what I'd always loved about him was his mind.

We walked gingerly to the backroom door and across the lab to the coat rack, where he helped me on with my raincoat and tied the crumpled kerchief under my chin to hide my frizzled head. My reflection in the glass of the front door- grizzled and be-kerchiefed—confirmed that I looked like my own grandmother. Bubby, we used to call her; I have no idea what her real name was. She spoke with an impenetrable Polish accent, despite the fact that she'd been in this country for fifty-seven years at the time of her death, and never went out without her babushka tied firmly under her chin. It was fitting that, twenty-five years younger in body, I found myself the spitting image of Bubby.

"Let's go," Frank said, holding me up as unobtrusively

as possible, as we shuffled down the hallway, out the front door, and across the parking lot to his Chevy Cavalier. I shivered inside my raincoat. The evening air had a chill to it, enough to take me by surprise. I looked around me: the trees were in blossom; the tulips and forsythia—even some renegade daffodils—were still in full flower. May 3, I thought, so cool and the forsythia's still out. I bet the Arctic's still frozen, the glaciers are intact, and the polar bears alive and well. Probably the Atlantic salmon population hasn't even crashed yet. Wow, 1987. It was nice to be back.

Frank opened the passenger door, sweeping an economy package of newborn-size Pampers off the front seat and into the back before he helped me in. He came around the car to the driver's side and sank down himself, turning towards me. All of a sudden he smiled, his face crinkling up the way it always did, and there it all was again: the hollows beneath prominent cheekbones, that wide expressive mouth, the fire in those dark blue eyes. Frank, just the way I remembered him, young, limber, sexy and in the flesh. I yearned to reach out and touch him, just to make sure he was real, but my arms wouldn't do what I asked them to.

It was only now that the magnitude of what had just happened flooded over me. I was here. This wasn't a memory. It was real. And not only had I accomplished what no one else ever had—if not in body then in mind—but I was back at a treasured time—the beginning of the best part of my life. Though Frank didn't yet know this, those four long breaths of life that he had just given me signified the beginning of our four-month-long affair. Perhaps it did not need to end in tragedy this time around.

Campus was the same and not the same. It seemed oddly lit until I realized it was just the absence of the high-intensity LED streetlights the university would install in 2009. Through some trees I hardly remembered, I could see a gap where the business building was yet to be, still the same old muddy lot of weeds and tire tracks until old Bachman died and left ten million dollars for its construction. The Arena was, of course, long in the future. In its place stood the old brick gym, tiny in comparison, its floor stained from use and with only bleachers for seats, hot in summer and cold in winter, and so poorly insulated that every wild shout and impassioned cheer could be heard in the street.

The students, faces just as young and shiny but seemingly less diverse, wore shoulder pads and big hair, leg warmers and stone washed jeans. And in their arms and in their book bags, they carried books! They talked to each other, two or three abreast, making full eye contact as they spoke. Social networks were the friends you could contact on your Rolodex. Life was what was before you, not what you saw on a little screen. It was hard to imagine a world without iPhones, without apps, without Facebook, but here it was.

Frank had by now started the motor, and headed off campus to downtown, the roads studded with old-fashioned street lights. I stared in wonder at Vinnie's Shoe Repair, Braun's Bakery, Peterson's Hardware, back like a dream after Bed, Bath and Beyond, Kohl's and Best Buy had long since taken their places. The solar panels that went in on the side of the road in 2010 had disappeared, rematerializing as telephone poles.

All I could do was observe. Nothing other than my right pinky finger was under my control, but my 35-year-old self seemed to be carrying on a lively monologue on what went wrong.

"The concept is sound," I was saying. "If Margaret at a particular instance in time is entangled with every other Margaret over time from birth to death, it remains theoretically possible that one can teleport the entangled particles from one instance to the other...."

Frank smiled but kept driving. He had heard it all before.

"It's got to be a simple mechanical failure. I'll fix it in the morning. I...."

"You'll be in the hospital tomorrow morning," Frank said. "It will have to wait until you're out."

"I'm perfectly fine. I'll be out in an hour."

Not quite an hour, I remembered. More like a four days, once the doctors took one look at me. And besides, we'd left the backroom unlocked and early the next morning the cleaning lady came in and....

"Margaret, you were practically electrocuted. We'll reset the date and do it as soon as you're up to it."

"Tomorrow," I said.

"You've got all the time in the world," Frank said, smiling.

Then, "Frank, we didn't lock the backroom door!"

"You're right," he said, his smile fading. "But I'll have to do it tomorrow. I've got to get home. I'm late already. Mimi is going to kill me. I told her I'd come home by five and spell her."

"Oh, yes. How's the baby?"

"Not sleeping. Isn't a newborn supposed to sleep all the time?"

"I wouldn't know. I don't know anything about babies. Frank," I said. "I'm really worried someone's going to come in and see the set-up in the backroom."

"Who? The cleaning lady?"

"No, really. Any of my grad students could come in anytime. And Caleb! He's always sneaking around. The moment I turn around, he's there...."

"It's six-thirty, Margaret," Frank said, pulling into the circle in front of the hospital. "If I know Caleb, he's in his den already pouring martinis. I'll lock the door first thing in the morning."

He stopped the car and turned to me, his arm slung over the back of the seat. There was something in the way he was looking at me, something electric in those blue eyes of his that made me want to throw myself into his arms. But neither he nor my alter ego seemed aware of what was about to happen. "You really don't look good, Margaret,"

Frank said suddenly. "Maybe I should walk you in."

"Aren't you expected at home?" I asked, pulling down the visor to look at myself. Bubby stared back. I pretended to fix a few grizzled strands of hair escaping the babushka. "How do I look now?" I asked, turning toward him, a goofy smile on my face.

At this, both of us began to laugh hysterically, way out of proportion to the silly joke, on and on until all the tension, fear and frustration had evaporated into little bubbles and effervesced up and out of our bodies.

"You really scared the hell out of me," Frank said, at last, taking his arm off the back of the seat and bringing his hand to rest on my arm. "You weren't breathing."

I looked back into the navy blue of his eyes. "Thank you for the kiss, by the way," I said softly. "It saved my life."

And, just as I remembered it, we gazed longingly at each other for another minute, oblivious to the cars piling up in the circle in back of us. Finally, Frank threw caution to the winds and kissed me, not in four long breaths as before, but long and hard and forever, while the cars honked in back of us.

CHAPTER 4

I GOT OUT A LITTLE unsteadily, walked around the car to the pavement, and watched Frank drive away. If I had anything to do with it, I would have hailed a taxi and gone back to the campus parking lot. Coming here, I knew, would hurt a lot more than it would help. But 35 had command, and I have to confess, I wasn't feeling so good. So, with the glass of the revolving door supporting me as I made my way around it, I entered the hospital. The waiting room was full of babies crying, a man with a swollen, purple leg, one old woman hobbling along, an even older man at her side. I ignored the pandemonium, putting all my energy into placing one foot in front of the other and managed to reach the other side of the room.

The woman at the front desk did a double-take when she saw me weaving my way across the lobby. She waved me around the counter to a glass enclosed space on the other side. "Sit down, please," she said, obviously worried that if I didn't sit down I might fall down.

She called up something on her computer screen, her fingers pecking at the keyboard. I craned my neck around to get a better look. It was the old DOS prompt, that little pointer asking for a user command! Man, I hadn't seen that in a donkey's years. No mouse to be seen, and a behemoth console which must have extended back a foot at least, atop a long flat rectangle with a slot for floppies. Floppies! I wondered what kind of chip that big beige box would have held back in '87. A first generation Pentium? A 486? I could hardly imagine it, but maybe, maybe a 386? How absolutely quaint.

"What happened?" the woman asked, her fingers poised above the keyboard.

"Happened?" I said, so caught up in the moment I had forgotten what I had come for.

"An accident?" she asked. "An explosion?"

Obviously, I wasn't going to tell the truth. That was one thing 35 and I both agreed upon. "My hair dryer short-circuited," I said, removing the kerchief. It seemed as close as I was going to get to the truth without giving them information they didn't need to know.

The clerk gasped at the sight but dutifully input the data into her computer. "How do you feel?" she asked.

"A little dizzy," I said.

"Nausea? Headache?"

"A little of both."

"Did you lose consciousness?"

Say no, I told myself. It's just going to get you in more trouble. "Um, yes," I said.

The clerk looked up. "Did you stop breathing?"

Under no condition should you say yes, I told myself. "Briefly," I replied.

This was like having locked-in syndrome, able to think just fine but unable to move or talk.

The clerk looked worried. "Do you have anyone here with you?"

"No," I said.

"You didn't drive yourself, did you?" the clerk scolded.

I held my figurative breath.

"Of course, not," I said aloud. "I took a taxi."

"Well, you should have someone to take you home. It sounds to me like you suffered a concussion, but we should rule out anything worse," the clerk said. "I'm sending your paperwork on to emergency. Can you walk there?"

I had a brief sensation of dizziness, but fought it off. "Absolutely."

Meanwhile, she had corralled a brawny young man in blue, who grabbed me by the shoulder and strong-armed me down a hallway toward *Triage*, in the end depositing me in a small cubicle with a hospital bed and sink with instructions to take off my clothes and put on a skimpy blue gown with the opening in the back. I waited until a young Indian woman in a white coat came in, her name tag identifying her as R. Jain, MD. There we went through the same questions and answers before she had me climb up on the bed.

This was all very familiar, even though it had happened twenty-five years ago. In fact, it was unnerving to relive something that had happened before, exactly as it happened and with no ability to change it. Morgan's complaint of 'I'd like to feel I'm free to live my life any way I choose' came to mind. I felt like telling the doctor to mind her own business and to call me a taxi, but 35 was much more amenable, no doubt because she didn't know what the future held.

"This is quite a burn," Dr. Jain was saying, touching the tattoo of a watchband on my left wrist. "All this from a hairdryer?"

"It short-circuited," I said again, wincing.

"You should notify the manufacturer."

I promised I would as soon as I got home.

"Of course, we'll have to keep you here for tests and observation," the doctor said, checking out the rosy hue from my neck to my waist.

And so it went. I was there for four days and had blood tests, EKGs and a full body CT scan. The blood tests hurt like hell, because they couldn't find a good vein, and the CT scan was like being buried alive, and anyway, everything was negative, something I could have told them before they started. Meanwhile, I was more or less incarcerated till they finished their series of tests which told no one anything. I would have emailed all of my students that class was cancelled, but email hadn't been invented yet outside of a few early networks. So I left a phone message with the department secretary telling her only that I'd be out several days and to let my students know. Frustratingly, I couldn't even tell them how long it would be because 35 did the talking, and she didn't know herself.

They stuck me in a double room the size of a walk-in closet and of a color so nondescript I couldn't tell whether it was green or blue or gray. Two beds were wedged into the little space, the one closer to the window already claimed by my roommate, a swarthy older woman with a tube up her nose and an air of misery. The window ledge had been crammed with cards, potted plants, and a helium balloon, emblazoned with "Get Well Soon Mom," that was tethered to the window crank. There was no space left for a second set of cards, balloons and plants, but 35 didn't seem to care. That made sense, I guess, if you thought you'd be out the next morning.

The next morning around ten I got a frantic call from Frank, who had managed to get the phone call patched through to my double room. I got up first and pulled the privacy curtain all around the bed. "Hello, Frank," 35 answered in a sultry voice, on the assumption that this would be a romantic interlude.

But it was obviously not a social call. "Margaret," he said right off. "I'm sorry, but the cleaning woman got into your lab before I did."

"No!" I shouted, to the chagrin of my roommate, who was trying to sleep after having been woken up every hour on the hour during the night by the on-duty nurse. "Did she see anything in the backroom?"

"She must have seen the whole set-up, though what she made of it, I don't know. She called Security, and they tried to get a hold of you at home, but when they couldn't, they called Joliet."

"What did I tell you," I said.

"And Joliet, when he couldn't find you anywhere, told the police."

"Wonderful."

"And somehow the campus newspaper found out, so don't be surprised if some reporter accosts you the moment you get out."

Just as I had feared, the whole business would soon be public knowledge. I only hoped we could still keep Frank out of the picture. "But, you, Frank," I said. "No one knows of your involvement, right?"

"No, but…"

"No buts. You were not involved."

"You better believe I'm involved," Frank said, more intimately.

I laughed. "Well, only in that way. But don't say anything to anyone. I'll handle it when I get out."

"When is that?"

I tried to form the words 'Saturday at noon,' but forget about that. 35 said, "A few days. They're still doing tests."

"How are you feeling?"

"I'm fine. No more dizziness. By the way, I told them my hairdryer short-circuited."

Frank laughed. "Nice try. Unfortunately, the department already knows it was more than that. Joliet's called a department meeting for Monday morning, assuming you're out of the hospital."

I'll be out, I thought. And I remember just how it went.

◊

I REJECTED THE WHEELCHAIR DEPARTURE down to the lobby, despite the nurse's insistence that insurance required that I be wheeled all the way to the front door. I've always suspected that they don't care what happens to you after they push you through that door. What matters is that you don't fall over and have a stroke in their lobby, and sue them for all their worth. A taxi can run you over in the front circle, but then you're no longer their responsibility. Anyway, I refused the whole farce and took the elevator myself down to the lobby.

Unfortunately, as Frank had predicted, there was the reporter for the *Garriston News:* a young coed in big hair, tight neon legwarmers under a miniskirt and an oversized sweater. She was holding a notebook and pencil, something I hadn't seen for some time, and standing just far enough back so that she could survey all three elevator doors at once. The moment I stepped out, she was all over me. Janie Carr I think her name was. She was the only one there, but from the frenzy of her movements, I could have sworn there were three of her.

"Dr. Braverman!" she cried, running straight to me. "Are you all right? Was there an explosion? What kind of experiment have you been conducting up in your lab at the university?"

As I remember, Janie is a very dangerous young woman to tangle with. Nothing I say will make any difference. What she doesn't know, she makes up.

"No comment," I said, trying to move past her, but she kept up.

"I can't help but notice that your hair is singed," she said, still at my side. "Did it have anything to do with that machine you keep in the back office?"

I seem to remember saying no comment time after time, across the lobby, through the revolving door, and on the pavement outside. It didn't have any effect the first time. I assumed that nothing would change this time either.

"Did it misfire? What was the intent of the experiment?"

"No comment."

We passed the coffee shop, half a dozen sleepy people perched at high round tables, drinking from large steaming cups, looking on.

"Did you have an assistant?"

"No comment."

The gift shop rushed by.

"The plug was pulled out of the wall. How did you manage to shut it off yourself?"

"No comment."

We were now at the revolving door. I managed to slide into a compartment alone, but Janie followed in the next one, the door ejecting her onto the pavement next to me.

"Taxi!" I called out. A red and white cab began its ascent from the bottom of the hill.

"Dr. Braverman," Janie began, positioning herself between the approaching cab and myself. "You had an assistant, didn't you? You must have. Who was it who helped you to shut the machine off?"

This time, my eye on the approaching taxi, I didn't even bother answering.

"Tell me, Dr. Braverman," Janie said, confidentially, her pencil poised above her pad. "Wasn't it really a *time* machine?"

I could feel the shock to my system: that shot of adrenalin that pours into your bloodstream when the very thing you feared comes to pass. I felt it because 35 had been taken by surprise, not that I hadn't been expecting that very question. It was an interesting sensation, like standing behind a lectern in front of a large audience. Although you know the material cold and there is really no cause for alarm, your heart is palpitating, your throat is dry, and your hands are trembling. In short, your body is acting as if a tiger were in hot pursuit, which is not true, and has nothing to do with presenting your speech on a two-state quantum-mechanical system, but there is little or nothing you can do to convince it otherwise. Meanwhile all you want is for your voice to stop quavering long enough to just deliver the stupid talk and move on to the wine and cheese afterwards.

The cab slid into the space in front of the revolving door and stopped. I sidled around the reporter and opened the back door. "I'll tell you what I told the doctors," I said, getting in. "My hair dryer short-circuited."

◊

As Frank had predicted, if I were out of the hospital by Monday, there would be a department meeting. And there was, worse than the one three years ago; more judgmental, more acrimonious, just as I remembered it. Dr. Joliet presided, his avuncular manner undone by hints of scandal and the beginning of that prostate cancer he didn't even know he had.

"Will the Physics Department come to order?" he growled.

As I had remembered, there was Dr. Joliet, Frank and me, Caleb, Edwin Royce, Walter Maxwell, and Henri D'Amboise. What I'd forgotten was that there was also a motley mix of assistant professors and instructors, who came and went, all relatively young men in chinos and corduroy jackets with patches on their sleeves. And there was Dana Michaelson, the only other woman in the department, fortyish and frumpy in a long pleated kilt and shapeless sweater, who always got saddled with the sec tions of Physics 101 for non-majors. I couldn't help but stare at each of them in turn, enthralled at the reincarnation of so many long-gone ghosts.

I hadn't seen Dana in years. I think she must have gotten sick and tired of always picking up the leftovers: teaching nights, evenings and summer sessions with little or no chance of tenure. I wondered what had happened to her. She must have left in the nineties sometime, but, for the moment, here she was right in front of me, before the burn out and the resentment, with that kind face and throaty laugh I had almost forgotten.

Henri D'Amboise, astrophysics, sat to her left. He'd

been such a star when he was first hired—actually stolen from Harvard for our endowed chair. We'd all sat in on the interview, in awe of his status, his accomplishments, the depth and musicality of his magnificent voice. He'd stayed with us the five years for which the chair was funded, and then was stolen away in turn by some other university more willing to bank-roll his celebrity. Henri sat back in his chair, hands behind his head, resplendent as usual in his red vest and striped tie, as big as life.

To his left sat Walter Maxwell, computational physics and the factotum of the department, the one who sent out the notices, sought out people in the hall to remind them of this or that. Power behind the scenes, maybe, but certainly no *éminence grise*. I couldn't believe it! Just the other day he was old and gray and all used up, but here was the Walter of a quarter century past, impossibly young, his hair still mouse brown and his skin unlined.

Across the table from Walter sat Edwin Royce, nuclear physics. Short, pale and wiry, hair the color of wheat, with no eyebrows to speak of, Edwin looked meek and mild-mannered. Anything but; even then, he was our own political firebrand. Well, no change here, despite the years. All that was missing was his iPhone.

And, of course, there was Caleb, atomic physics, one seat down from Dr. Joliet. Forty pounds lighter than when he barged into my office the day before, his soft round face no longer sported the broken blood vessels and bulbous nose brought about by twenty-five years of serious drinking. That baby face didn't fool me, however. Caleb was a mean-spirited, conceited, womanizing, step-on-your-mother's-face-to-get-ahead-if-necessary obnoxious little prick. And anything I could do this time around to thwart his plans to be department chair, you bet I was up for it.

And then there was Frank, theoretical physics, up for tenure later that year though no one questioned whether he would get it, because he was generally agreed to be an engaging teacher as well as a researcher with a lot of potential and great scope. It was incidentally for those very reasons that Caleb hated him, the envy in his eyes flashing green each time Frank got another grant. If there were any way he could figure out how to prevent Frank from getting tenure Caleb would do it with a complete lack of remorse.

Frank was sitting way down at the bottom of the table, in stiff new jeans, with a Madras shirt and a wild tie, averting his eyes when I came in. From the look on his face, I could tell he was nervous about how to play this thing. How could he support me without letting on that he was part of it? Good old Frank, who couldn't lie to save his life.

We met in the old conference room, the one with the blackboard and the old 3M overhead projector. No wireless, no telephone conferencing capabilities: just us and a long shiny table, the Mr. Coffee urn and a box of Dunkin' donuts set on a tea cart in the corner. Bare and minimal, but new and shiny, just as we all were then. In my dreams, and believe me I had had many of this day, it was never so vivid, so tangible. The aroma of freshly brewed coffee filled my senses, along with the flash of sunbeams through the window. There was the squeak of molded plastic chairs on the new linoleum floor, punctuated by Dana Michaelson's throaty laugh; that nauseating green color of the walls; the shiny wood surface of the table; the easy responsiveness of young fit muscles; the satisfying inhalation of oxygen into my lungs. I don't think I had ever felt as alive as today.

"This is a special meeting of the department, so I think we can dispense with the review of old business and go directly on to the one piece of new business that we are calling this meeting to discuss," Dr. Joliet said, gazing meaningfully at me. "And that, of course, is to find out exactly what it was that happened in Dr. Braverman's lab on May 3."

I could feel everyone's eyes on my grizzled hair and barbecued skin, but no one said a word.

"Margaret," Dr. Joliet said. "Might we have an explanation?"

The room was quiet, waiting for my answer. I stood up and faced them all. I had decided to make a clear breast of it and let the chips fall where they might.

"Mr. Chairman and all my fellow physicists," I said. "I cannot lie to you. Based on both a long meditation on the nature of space-time and that of quantum entanglement, I managed to build a time machine."

A shocked pause and then the room erupted in a low buzz of laughter and derision.

Dr. Joliet stood up slowly and solemnly raised his right hand for quiet. "I have asked Dr. Braverman a question. Please be good enough to let her answer."

I took a breath and started again. "We all know that conventional entanglement acts across space, linking particles instantly in time. But why couldn't entanglement just as easily act across time, linking particles in space? What, I thought, if two particles were separated in time but situated at exactly the same place? Couldn't one teleport across vast distances of time?"

Caleb pushed his chair back and laughed. "Even if that were true, you'd never be able to send anything larger than a quantum bit. The laws of Thermodynamics forbid it."

"But what if one were to send one's conscious self?" I asked, ignoring the comment. "It emerges out of the quantum world but is something entirely different. Neither quantum nor classical, micro nor macro, matter nor energy, it belongs to a level of substance with its own laws."

Walter from his chair muttered, "I think she's lost her mind in the explosion."

"An instance of that mind sent from a single place in the present to the exact same place in the future?" I continued, ignoring him, too.

Dr. Joliet, who had been controlling himself mightily in the interest of open-mindedness, could not help but stand up again. "Very interesting concept to be sure, but I must remind you that your experiment was a failure."

"Oh, but it was just a glitch," I replied, laughing. "A

mere mechanical problem. I assure you it will work the next time I try it."

More buzz, punctuated by gasps and a loud laugh.

"Oh, but you won't be trying it again," Dr. Joliet told me.

I planted both hands on my hips in a classic gesture of defiance and said, "Won't I, then."

"If you plan to, Dr. Braverman, you can be sure we'll confiscate that ridiculous machine first."

"You can't interfere with my research," I shouted, turning my head to stare every member of the department in the eye, ending with Frank, whose face was contorted in what looked like pain. "This is a matter of academic freedom."

"It's not academic freedom if it's false science ," Dr. Joliet replied. "And we will do what we have to, Margaret, in the event you are in any danger of harming yourself."

I sat down, or rather fell down into my chair. I had never really thought that Joliet was afraid of my harming myself. He was more worried about bold newspaper headlines charging Garriston U's Physics Department with doing nothing to prevent a young professor from electrocuting herself. In any case, nothing I could do or had done would make a difference. I know that now.

Suddenly, at the far end of the table, Frank's voice spoke up. "I'm ashamed of all of us. We're supposed to be scientists: willing to entertain new notions, not reject them out of hand or blackmail our fellow scientists into submission.

"Who's to say that the laws of the incorporeal mind don't have more in common with the quantum world than the world we know? Who's to say that the mind cannot go backwards or forwards in time, like the quantum stuff from which it is made? Or that the particles that compose it cannot be hopelessly entangled in time with the self they once were?"

A dozen voices rose to cut him off, but Frank shouted them down. "I for one feel that if it can be done, it will be done. Truth will out. If the hypothesis is false, then it will eventually be disproven. But give it a chance! As silly as most of you think Margaret's hypothesis is, she deserves the right to prove it one way or the other."

As he sat down, I had a strong urge to stand up and applaud him, but he had already gone out on a limb for me, and I didn't want to call any more attention to the fact. In any event his gallantry would accomplish nothing; their minds were closed and padlocked. Dr. Joliet stood up again and reminded me that we had had this same talk three years before, and that I'd promised then that if I were ever to aspire to tenure I would have to agree to give up all this ridiculous speculation about time travel, and that I had promised. The Department had done its part in awarding me tenure, and the agreement still held.

I remembered back to the first meeting three years ago, and how Frank came up to me afterwards to tell me that unlike Dr. Joliet, he thought very highly of out-of-the-box thinking. He asked me to coffee where we discussed all matter of consciousness, time travel, and far-out speculation. In fact, over the next few years these free spirited discussions led to our theory of entanglement over time, a strong but platonic relationship, and the secret construction of our backroom machine. And, well, you know the rest.

◊

I DON'T KNOW WHY, BUT when someone tells me I can't do something, I can't seem to stop myself from trying. And I never give up, because something deep inside me says that there is a right answer to every question. If I just work hard enough, I'll find it.

I've always loved science. I loved it in grade school where science meant collecting leaves and pasting them in a scrap book or making a volcano erupt onto your desk using baking soda, dish soap, and vinegar. I loved it in middle school when it meant a home-made telescope and A Day in Your Digestive System. I loved it in high school when it meant DNA, superconductivity and dissecting frogs.

I loved the order behind it all: the way equations showed a universe that was all of one piece, run by glorious unifying laws that governed time and space and light and life, not some chaotic mess of unrelated details and random instances that signified nothing. Facts and figures were nothing to me, but the fitting them together piece by piece into some giant jigsaw puzzle that, when completed, made sense of it all—that was everything.

I remember—I couldn't have been more than eight. My grandfather had died, and we were just back from the cemetery. He was a wonderful man, who used to keep a set of magic tricks in his roll-top desk to beguile us children, and whenever we walked together on the street, miraculously discovered quarters and nickels and dimes beneath our feet. Not till long afterwards did I figure out his sleight of hand in palming those coins, so seamless was Grandpa's magic.

After the funeral, I went upstairs and lay down on my bed and cried. The thought of never seeing him again was so unutterably sad. Where did he go? How can someone be and then not be? The earth seemed to open up into a bottomless void. Then, just as quickly, I laughed, because it was suddenly crystal clear to me how that this thing we called life was just an illusion, and so was death. The answer was somehow in the magical unity of them, though being material the way I was, I couldn't see the whole of it. Grandpa wasn't gone. He was hiding in plain sight.

Einstein imagined himself riding on a light beam and all at once knew that light was the absolute and time was relative. The chemist Kékulé dreamt of a snake coiled and biting its tail and recognized it then and there as the molecular structure of benzene. Archimedes, getting into a pool in a public bathhouse, all of a sudden intuited that the volume of an object equaled the amount of water it displaced. He leapt out of the pool and ran home, naked, crying, Eureka, eureka! I found it!

There's a split second when you understand the universe, when a solution comes to you and you don't know how or why. Call it intuition; call it inspiration, but suddenly everything comes together, and it is a thing of beauty.

CHAPTER 5

I REMEMBER WALKING, HEAD DOWN, out of that first department meeting—the one where Dr. Joliet made me promise never to mention time travel in body or mind again. That would have been 1984, I guess: three years ago, judging by my current now, or twenty-eight from my future now. Either way it's the past, just the angle is a little different. For 35, I figure, recalling this would probably be like shoving a book so close to your face that the words blur in front of one's eyes. For me, 60, from the point of view of close to thirty years, the whole thing's crystal-clear. Sometimes you just need a little perspective.

A few steps out the door, as I remember, Frank fell into step with me, a tall shadow to my left.

"Margaret," he said. "You have a free moment to discuss your theory with me?"

"You're not afraid to be seen with the pariah of the Garriston Physics Department?" I asked.

He laughed. "Actually, I thought you presented a very intriguing hypothesis in there. I congratulate you on your out-of-the-box thinking."

Uh-oh, I remember thinking. The guy thinks I'm a lunatic. "Anyway, thanks for standing up for me," I said.

"I wasn't just standing up for you. I find the topic fascinating. Do you want to discuss it further over a cup of coffee?" Frank asked again.

It was late afternoon, and my classes were finished for the day, so I agreed. I knew he was already in a relationship. At that point, it wasn't a sexual thing. I barely knew him, for God's sake. Maybe, I figured, he really did like out-of-the-box thinking.

I remember the two of us going two buildings over and a flight of stairs down to a little subterranean coffee shop informally called the dirty donut, though I doubt that that was its real name. In any case, it's been gone for years. Years from 2012, that is. For a time, I remember, it was a computer lab. The last I knew it was an annex for the library. But back in eighty-four, it was a place you could get a decent cup of coffee, and it was close.

Inside, despite the afternoon sun outdoors, it could have been midnight, the only light a dozen flickering votives, each set mid-table and spaced randomly around the room. The silhouette of a door on the far wall, backlit by a halo of light, together with a faint whiff of coffee, suggested there was a kitchen, perhaps even food and drink. A musty dampness seeped in from the cement floor. As my eyes adapted, a chalk board on the wall came into focus, the day's specialty coffees and teas spelled out in chalk. Cappuccino, it said. Espresso. Regular brew. Lipton's Tea. Donut of the day: (rubbed out, then written on top) chocolate glazed.

The kitchen door opened, and a small figure in a cap and apron, silhouetted against a blaze of light, beckoned us to sit down anywhere. Frank chose a table in the corner, and we sat. The waitress said her name was Emily and claimed to be a sophomore, though I seem to remember her looking as if she were sixteen. Everyone looks like that to me now, but this was when I was 32, so I suspect she really did look that young. She asked us what we wanted.

"Regular coffee. With cream," Frank said. "And your special—the chocolate glazed donut. Margaret, what'll you have?"

"Just coffee, thanks." No request for decaf, of course, mostly because in those days I slept like a log no matter how much caffeine I poured into myself. Also, because in eighty-four, if you wanted decaf, they'd have brought you a cup of hot water with a little orange packet of instant Sanka, the blending of which resembled coffee about as much as Tang resembled orange juice.

Emily pushed back through the swinging door, the sudden explosion of light from the kitchen flashing a quick snapshot of the room into my eyes: twelve dinged wooden tables covered in brown butcher paper; a few dozen mismatched chairs encircling them; cinderblock walls painted almost smooth with untold layers of old enamel; Frank squinting, dazzled by the light. Then the door closed and we were left blinking in the dark.

Just as our eyes readapted to candlelight, the kitchen door banged open again, blinding us. A pair of disembodied hands placed two mugs and a plate down in front of us.

"Enjoy," Emily said, banging back through the blazing door.

"So," Frank said after the room had stabilized again. Orange shadows from the votive candle played across Frank's face, bringing out the angle of the cheek bones, the wide expanse of brow, and illuminating the little fan of smile lines around the eyes. "Tell me about your time machine."

I took a long, slow sip of coffee. Frank seemed serious and sympathetic. Perhaps, I thought, he was. In any case, there was no one else, and I could use a sympathetic ear. I decided to take a chance.

I began by telling him about my initial inspiration. How it started with the idea of two particles at different sides of the universe but entangled in space. How one particle uncannily could transmit information to the other in no time at all. "What one knows," I said, "the other instantaneously knows, even if the two are light years away from each other."

That was the standard definition of entanglement: Nothing new here. Frank nodded.

"Of course," I went on, "such a thing can't occur in our everyday world. There's no viable way a body can go through time in this way. But the mind, well, that might just be different. I envisage entangling two discrete conscious states, from the same individual but...."

Frank's face, which had been looking steadily more skeptical, suddenly erupted into a laugh. "But how could entanglement possibly exist between whole conscious states, Margaret?" he protested. "People are not on/off. We can't resolve them into single states."

I answered that synchronous firing of neurons in different regions of the brain was a well-known explanation underlying the binding of the mind into a single moment of consciousness.

"That's just a theory, Margaret," Frank said, putting his coffee cup down with a bang and a splash. "And a simplistic one at that. My God, there's something like a hundred billion nerve cells alone. How could it all function as if it were a single particle?"

"It doesn't matter how many parts are in the whole," I interrupted. "The whole thing ends up bound into a single synchronous state. A single state."

For a moment there was a silent stand-off. "They're all bound together, you're saying," Frank said at last, folding his arms in front of his chest.

"Yes," I said.

"Billions of nerve cells in sync with each other, networks in sync with other networks, and networks of networks, ad infinitum?" he said, not sounding like he believed it at all.

"Yes," I said.

I remember feeling that I was losing him. Frank had started out with an open mind, but his folded arms and snarky responses told me in no uncertain terms that he was beginning to agree with his fellow colleagues. She's a little touched in the head, I figured he was thinking.

Frank unfolded his arms. "Okay," he said. "Let's say, just for the sake of argument, that the mind can be treated as a single particle state. Not that I accept it, mind you. Just for the sake of argument. Then what you're saying is that each of these single states can be entangled with a future state of the same mind, but a different time."

"Exactly," I said.

For the next minute, as we sipped in silence, I watched him covertly over my coffee cup. There was that sexy charisma he radiated when he looked at me intently, his hair kind of falling into his eyes, without his even bothering to push it back; the blue intensity of those eyes, which seemed to pierce the darkness when he argued; the crinkly lines when he smiled. But, I reminded myself, he already had a girlfriend.

"Are you saying that each conscious moment is entangled with the one which follows it?" he said after a long pause.

It wasn't quite what I meant. "No," I told him. "I'm saying that a conscious state can be entangled with another in the same person but many years apart."

He took a long meditative sip. "You're not talking standard entanglement in space, then."

"No," I told him. "I'm talking about entanglement in time."

Well, that seemed to get to him. His eyes seemed to internalize the flame from the candle as he sat back and refolded his arms across his chest. I watched the flame in his eyes as he thought.

"But entanglement has only been theorized to work

over space," Frank finally said, sitting forward again. "And, even there, that's been proven mathematically but never actually experimentally demonstrated."

"It'll be demonstrated eventually," I remember replying. Of course, it would be—I myself demonstrated entanglement in space just months ago—in 2012. And the original proof of entanglement in time was published in 2011 by Olson and Ralph.

But at the time, I didn't know any of that. My conviction was just fueled by intuition and conceit. Oh, yes, conceit. As my father so often said, Margaret never listened to anyone else but herself. In those days, I didn't think I needed to.

"You have some mathematical proof for this?" Frank asked.

Proof? I remember thinking that I'd trust my own intuition any day over anyone else's proof. "No," told him. "The whole thing was an epiphany."

Then Frank laughed. He had to stop himself from snorting up the coffee into his nose, he laughed so much. "Well," he finally said, wiping his eyes with a paper napkin. "You need a proof. At least proof of concept. You can't just postulate anything you want, even if you did have an epiphany."

"I figured I'd do the math afterwards," I told him. Or, perhaps, someone else—the Walters of the world—could do the proving. There were the idea people, like me, and then there were the numbers people who served to test and demonstrate and prove someone else's ideas. I didn't need to lower myself by working out all the little details. My intuition was right.

But for the first time I wondered—briefly—whether it was.

"Oh, Margaret," Frank said, still laughing. "That's way too sloppy. Epiphanies can just go so far; you've got to ...." He stopped suddenly as if something had hit him in the head. "Mmm. Interesting, though. If there's entanglement of particles over space, who's to say it couldn't be over time? Just reverse the axes. ... ."

I could almost hear the clink-clank of machinery in Frank's mind: the wheels turning, gears grinding, components snapping together into new, unheard-of configurations, the whole mechanism tumbling and twisting until that aha moment when CLICK! every piece locks into place.

He placed his mug on top of the plate and to the side of the remaining half donut, and pushed the whole thing over to the edge of the table, clearing a large central space.

"Let's begin by thinking about a simplified universe consisting of one dimension of space and one of time," Frank said, reaching down into the front pocket of his briefcase for a felt-tip pen. He began to sketch something out on the paper tablecloth. Upside down, I watched him draw the axes of a graph: a vertical one, x, for space, and a horizontal one, y, for time.

"Imagine," he said as he drew, "the present as the

origin—where the two axes meet. Then the future—the space you can reach at speeds of less than the speed of light—forms a wedge to the right of the x-axis, where time is positive. The past is the mirror image of this wedge but to the left of the x-axis, where time is negative."

Upside down and in the dark, it wasn't easy to see, but, yes, I saw two sets of wedges in the area above the y axis, one set to the right, and one set to the left. Nothing was in the lower half of the graph, where space was negative, if there were such a thing.

"Now, conventional entanglement acts along the x-axis," Frank went on, drawing his finger up and down along the axis of space. "So, it links particles instantly in time, regardless of whether they are in the future wedge or the past wedge of space."

I nodded. I couldn't help but be distracted by two not-so-symmetrical wet coffee rings, like two minor planets in a brown-paper sky, but I was pretty sure that I was supposed to overlook those.

"Yet, entanglement can just as easily work along the y-axis, too," Frank said, gesturing along the axis of time, "so that it links particles in space, regardless of where they are in time."

He paused to let this sink in before giving me the final judgment. "At least theoretically, Margaret, you should be able to send your quantum mind state into the future without traversing the middle time."

Frank had me hold the plate with his mug as he slid

the paper tablecloth around so that it faced me. Despite the two coffee rings, I could see exactly what he meant. Frank had, on the fly, sketched out a conceptual proof of entanglement over time.

There was a sparkle in his eyes that wasn't there before, the sparkle of excitement. I figured I had it, too. "Wow," I remember saying. "I can't believe you worked the whole thing out in ten minutes." This wasn't just blindly plugging numbers into other people's theories. There was brilliance there. Vision, even. What a team we could make.

CHAPTER 6

AFTER THE SECOND DEPARTMENT meeting, Frank and I didn't talk again for a few days. We'd pass each other on campus, but I figured that it would be better to let this whole thing die down before we were seen together socially. Still, I couldn't get him out of my mind. Occasionally, at eleven o'clock in the morning on Tuesdays and Thursdays, I'd sneak down two floors from my lab and spy in on him through the window of the classroom door housing Physics 223. With the vacuum-sealed construction of the science building, I couldn't hear a thing, but I could observe Frank sitting on the corner of the desk talking animatedly or perhaps striding around, gesturing as he paced. I could tell when he told a joke, because the class, a mix of equal genders—a wonder in physics where the usual was ninety percent male—would erupt in silent laughter. Every face was trained on his, the usual expression one of rapt attention and, in the case of the girls, doe-eyed adoration. I'd stand there for fifteen minutes or so, no doubt with my own lovelorn expression, until I managed to tear myself away and go back to work.

Caleb, on the other hand, seemed to pop up everywhere. Nothing prevented him from materializing in the lunch room, in the hallway, or right in back of me whenever I turned around. He may not have thought much of me as a physicist, but he made it pretty clear what he thought of me as a woman. Every Christmas party I had to fight off his drunken advances. And then there was the assault in my lab that I'd rather not think about. I'd considered filing a formal complaint for stalking or harassment, but you didn't do that in those days, not, at least, if you were a woman in a mostly male physics department and not if you were not prepared to sacrifice your career.

In any case, here he was again, coming into my office, this time his hand wrapped around the newest copy of the *Garriston News.* Funny how the scene seemed vaguely familiar.

Caleb held out the newspaper, the headline reading, **Garriston student overturns car in campus parking lot.** I couldn't quite figure why he'd be coming all the way over to my office just to show me this, but, okay, I read on....

Three Garriston University students avoided serious injury when their car hit a lamppost and overturned on campus yesterday, the police said. Rhonda Novak, 19, of Somerset was turning around in a parking lot behind the athletic field when she became distracted, jumped the curb and hit the light post. Novak, Leanne Rhodes, 21, and Patricia Cappacchio, 20, all with minor bruises, managed to crawl out of the sunroof, Sergeant Morland said.

"Sorry, is this the article you wanted me to read?" I asked, indicating the picture of a lamppost bent into a surreal shape beside an overturned car.

Caleb craned his neck to see where I was pointing. "You wish," he said, his finger descending the page to another, smaller font.

Mysterious Accident in Physics Lab, it read. Underneath, an old photo of me in cap and gown smiled out at the reader.

But before I could read any of it, Caleb pulled the paper back and began to read aloud. "In response to the question of whether the strange machine found in the normally locked backroom wasn't 'really a time machine,' Dr. Braverman, her hair singed and her skin burned a dark red in places, claimed, 'My hair dryer short-circuited.'"

"That's a run-on sentence," I said.

Caleb dropped down into the visitor's chair, chuckling. He unfolded the paper to page two. "Interesting picture they have here of your 'hair dryer'."

I sighed. "Okay, what is it you want, Caleb?"

His baby face looked stung. "You really know how to hurt a guy, Margaret. I just came in to commiserate with you."

"Thanks, but I don't need any. I've got all the misery I can use."

Caleb cracked a smile but didn't move. "You know, this reporter, um," he said, looking back at the first page, "this Janie Carr came to see me yesterday."

I knew all about this, of course, but 35 didn't, and gave quite a start.

"Yeah," Caleb said, grinning at my reaction. "She asked me all sorts of questions."

"Really?" I said. "Like?"

"Really. Like what your research was about, whether the department knew about this. Whether they supplied a lab assistant."

"I see," I said.

"What I answered was, one, mostly particle physics, but what was in the backroom seemed to be outside that realm. Two, the department had not known about this and three...." He paused, looking up at me. "What should I have told her, Margaret? Did you have an assistant?"

"What did you answer?" I asked, my body trembling.

"I told her I would ask you, of course." Caleb said, smiling. "And get back to her."

"Well, I did it all alone," I said.

"Right," Caleb said, getting up. "Just like your hair dryer short-circuiting."

As I said, Caleb is a mean-spirited, conceited, womanizing, step-on-your-mother's-face-to-get-ahead-if-necessary obnoxious little prick, and someone should have told him so. But 35 was speechless, and so was I.

◊

THE FOLLOWING DAY, FROM my seventh floor perch in the science building, I watched as Facilities hummed about outfitting the quad with a thousand seats around a large platform. It took them an hour alone to string the banner up behind the dais. "Garriston U welcomes Vice President Bush," it now said in blue and red, the college colors. Another hour or two it took to strategically place podium, lights and awning, and three more to line up the chairs in military precision.

The event, ostensibly a speech on U.S.-Soviet relations, had been advertised for the past two weeks, and by now the loud grumblings about Iran-Contra were threatening to overshadow the speech itself. What did Bush know about the channeling of covert profits from gun sales to Iran over to the Nicaragua rebels, and how far up did this knowledge extend? Not a lot of people were there for the U.S. Soviet relations angle, of course. Most everyone was really going for the question period afterwards, when anyone could go off-topic and with any luck catch the VP in some egregious slip.

Whatever the true draw, University administration obviously felt that there would be an enormous turnout. Now, with an hour still to go, half the seats were already full, and curiosity seekers could be seen to be pouring in from every angle. I could just make out Janie Carr near the dais kibitzing with one of the many photographers. It looked like Channel 8 was in the mix.

Edwin had been on my case about abandoning the lab and going down to be part of it, but 35 gave him the usual schtick about having deeper things on one's mind than politics. Really, ever since the incident in my lab, it was hard enough keeping out of the local newspapers; I didn't need to turn up on Channel 8 as well. But Edwin never did let up. "History might be made," he told me cryptically; he'd gotten pledges from a big percentage of his students to come, and something was definitely coming off. But I didn't care. Protests, wars, power plays, covert arms deals. Ho-hum. I never did like politics. A birds-eye view on this particular spectacle was more than enough for me.

There, making his entrance onto the green, was Edwin, looking like the Pied Piper of Garriston, trailed as he was by a couple of dozen students. I could see him pointing out the way to a row way up in the front and watched the parade of students follow his finger, filing in one by one. Even by Edwin's standards, front row was quite a coup, I remember thinking the last time I was here. How, I wondered, did he ever manage that? It turned out, as I found out later, to be a political tit for tat, something that Edwin did so well. I'll wash your hands if you wash mine sort of thing. I can't remember whose hands he washed for this ringside seat, though.

Someone was busy setting up the microphone. I could make out one of the Facilities people speaking into it, fiddling with it, speaking again. Of course, I couldn't hear a thing, what with the soundproof, noiseproof, airproof qualities of the science building, but I had a panoramic view. People were streaming in by now: students, faculty, cafeteria workers, grounds people, coaches, librarians. The thousand folding chairs looked pretty well full. I glanced at my watch. Ten minutes to go.

Five to seven and bursting at the seams: not a single empty seat. I could tell the natives were getting restless, craning their necks to get the first glimpse of the secret service men fanning out along the platform. In the audience, Edwin was squatting in front of his entourage, giving them some sort of pep talk, but no one in or around the platform seemed to pay them any heed at all. From the standpoint of 2012, when grandmothers routinely get frisked at the airport, that was a surprise. But this was before 9/11, when we still—hahaha—thought nothing bad could happen on U.S. soil.

There. I could see the top of Bush's head as he headed for the platform, surrounded by a fan of secret service men who, ready for anything, could grab you and wrestle you down onto the ground, if you so much as made a move to reach for your comb from your inside jacket pocket.

Still, they seemed stymied by several of Edwin's students, who suddenly stood up, their arms raised in the Nazi salute. Now a couple were goose-stepping down the aisle, mocking Bush. Nothing dangerous. Nothing that would trigger the secret service men's conditioned reflexes. But insulting, for sure. I saw the whole thing later on Channel 8, complete with sound. Those goose-stepping students were saying, "Sieg Heil. Sieg Heil." What a disgrace, especially from the standpoint of 2012. Surely if there ever were a compassionate conservative, it was Bush the father.

The whole thing, I decided, was Edwin's doing. He'd

coached his students to be as disruptive as possible, anything to publicize their anger over U.S. support for the Contras, the rebels the Reagan administration supported with the illicit profits they made selling arms to Iran. It's not that I don't agree that the whole thing stunk to high heaven. It's just that Edwin always went about it the wrong way.

When Bush began to speak, they interrupted him throughout with catcalls, curses, and chants of "He's a terrorist," "Bullshit," and "Nazi." Before the event was over, University Police had arrested three students for disorderly conduct and dragged away three others for waving an obscene banner. But Bush kept on speaking. He ignored the protesters until the end, when the worst thing he could bring himself to say about them was that they were a "motley-looking group of people."

H.W. was really a good sort, so much more thoughtful than his son, W. And he was a better president, too. But not being Teflon like his boss, he got the blame. As I remember, Reagan admitted a few months later that policy went astray, and took responsibility. Too little, too late, but somehow, and despite the stock market crash of 1987, the scandals at the Environment Protection Agency, Nancy's $200,000 White House china, nothing stuck to him.

I guess he gave the people what they wanted—not economic trickle down the way he promised, but the illusion of pride and strength and triumph. Instead of broken Vietnam vets, he gave us Rambo. Instead of

Carter's "malaise" and peanut butter, he gave us hope and Hollywood. Smoke and mirrors to be sure, but the fact is that a lot of us believed him. We believed that getting rich was justified because it left the nation better off, and that cutting aid to the poor was humane because welfare hurt initiative. Somehow Reagan convinced two hundred million Americans, despite evidence to the contrary, that life was grand.

Except for certain campus activists like Edwin, who called Reagan a Nazi. Edwin stayed largely out of the limelight, but I always knew that he was the brains behind the demonstration. After all, who else would have dreamed up "Sieg Heil" as a protest? Though the Garriston President, Martin Cooley, apologized to Bush for the students' behavior, Edwin never apologized to anyone. That was just the way he was. "All's fair in love, war, and politics," he used to say. And still does, come to think of it.

◊

I HAD BOUGHT THE HOUSE in the anticipation of the money and recognition I was sure to get from the time travel experiment, and had told everyone I would have the department over as soon as I had gotten the place furnished. So, failure or not, rejection or not, I decided to go through with the housewarming. In fact, there may have been some unconscious method to my madness in having that party, who knows: part bribe, part suck-up, part Pollyanna hope that in bringing everyone together in my house, I would magically morph into a respectable member of Garriston

U's Physics Department.

Without departmental email, I distributed mimeographed invitations into everyone's mail cubicle. Surprisingly, no one said no. Perhaps morbid curiosity was the reason. Maybe people hoped to see me dematerialize at the kitchen table or sail around the living room on a broomstick. In any case, the attendees worked out to around twenty people: five wives, one husband, several significant others, along with all the usual department members. I went around making ice, polishing the *tchotchkas*, and setting out my grandmother's silverware. I split a dozen seasoned alder logs I'd found in the back with an axe I'd bought at the hardware store along with a batch of long wooden matches and a set of fireplace tools. I carried the logs in, in armfuls of twos and threes at a time, and arranged them into my notion of an ideal pyramid over crumpled balls of *Garriston News* underneath. But it wouldn't light, no doubt because it had rained the night before. Of course, I—60—had known all this would happen. I'd tried to take the wood in earlier, to convey the problem to my muscles if not my brain, to change the outcome in some practical way, but nothing seemed to make any difference. 35 and I were like two independent drivers of the same jalopy, but only she knew how to steer this gosh-darn thing, and only I could see the blessed road ahead. I wondered whether the two of us would ever connect.

A couple of hours before the party started, Frank staggered in carrying a big pot of chili. "Just keep it on a low flame," he said, placing it on a back burner, his eyes averted. "And it should be ready by the time everyone gets here."

I thanked him and walked him back to the front door. On the way, he took a look into my fireplace at my idealized log pyramid. Geek that he was, he couldn't resist offering to remake it into the teepee he had learned as a cub scout. I demurred. I could do it, I said. It was just simple physics. He shrugged and continued on, face determinedly pointed towards the door. He was still keeping a low profile, damn him, even though no one was there yet. I could feel the irritation build in me, the adrenalin rising, until finally, at the door, my emotions just couldn't take it anymore. Someone had to say something.

"Frank, it's no big deal," I huffed. "No one knows you were helping me. No one knows we kissed. No one except me, and I won't tell. Don't worry about it."

He turned toward me, his eyes finding mine for the first time since that day in the car. "It *is* a big deal. I'd tell the whole world if it were up to me. I'd tell them that I was there in body and soul." He paused before adding, "I'd tell them that I think I'm in love with you."

At that, I could feel a thrill of excitement go up my body, but I waited, because the second shoe was about to drop.

"But I can't act on any of it, Margaret," he said. "I'm sorry. I can't leave Mimi and the baby, and I won't jeopardize my livelihood because that would put them at risk, too." There was real sorrow in those dark eyes, some sexy mix of yearning and love and regret that made me want to throw my arms around him and squeeze my body against his, but I didn't.

"I shouldn't have ever kissed you in the first place," he conceded. "It was unforgivable of me when I knew I couldn't...," he said, his voice fading out as he caught the longing on my face. My hand rose on its own towards his cheek, and he bent towards me, lips closer and closer until he kissed me again, his arms drawing me in.

"That's the very last kiss," Frank said as we came up for air.

"The last one," I agreed.

I dropped onto the sofa after he had left, my heart galloping and a fire in my lower half. At thirty-five I hadn't had sex in oh, a couple of years, so it was natural that even the prospect of a good-looking man would get my undies into a knot. But the feeling at sixty was way beyond that. By then I hadn't had sex in, goodness, had it really been fifteen years? By then I'd given it up along with all the other good things in life—Frosted Flakes, say, or skinny dipping; strapless dresses or sleeping through the night; that second piece of cheesecake, or sex with the love of my life, not necessarily in that order. I was tired and a little bitter, dead sure that what I had accomplished wasn't half of what I'd expected of myself. I'd even lost the taste for life, or so I thought. But what was this yearning, burning feeling? Desire? And what was this fizzy feeling which made me want to giggle? Could it conceivably be joy? It had been so long I hardly recognized it.

I might have sat there rejoicing until my first guests appeared, except 35 wasn't nearly as blown away as I was, and there were things to be done. I got up and struck one of the long fireplace matches to a crumpled wad of *Garriston News*. It caught, and then another and another, all the paper flaming up merrily before it died, but the logs were something else entirely. I crumpled twice as much, stuffing it into the hot space between stone and wood, and struck another match. This time, with the paper on fire, I caught a hint of steam as it rose up from one of the damp logs. Half an hour and several lurid headlines later, I had, if not a roaring fire, a pile of ashes, a roomful of smoke and a few mildly glowing embers. It would just have to do.

I opened the window and turned down the flame under the chili, whose spicy aroma had by now permeated the house, adding that certain *je ne sais quoi* to the smoke in the living room. I put out the cheeses, the veggies, the breads and the pate and started the oven for the Bagel Bites I had just yesterday discovered in the freezer section of the supermarket as I was looking for quiche. I wasn't quite sure, but I had the liberating feeling that, as my fingers hovered over the box, their boss mind clearly deliberating over whether to buy this new, unproven product, I—Margaret 60—had weighed in just enough to grasp the package and tip it into the cart. It gives one hope.

I had barely enough time to dress and turn on the lights before the doorbell rang. It was Dana Michaelson in another of her trademark long kilts and shapeless sweaters, her spouse trailing with a foil-wrapped tray of lasagna. Then it rang again to a bunch of assistant professors and girl friends, one salad, a casserole, some beer; followed by Mark Schwartz, our newest hire, his boyfriend and a fancy rum cake.

"Mark!" I wanted to shout, maybe throw my arms around him if I could. He was oh so young and rather dashing, his brown hair thick and wavy, his eyes sparkling as he introduced his new boyfriend. Jerry looked fit and hunky in a muscle t-shirt under his blazer. God, the two of them looked so happy, healthy, young and beautiful. So unsoiled by life.

And then to Henri D'Amboise, a white silk scarf slung casually over his Harris Tweed jacket, carrying two bottles of Mouton Rothschild. Finally, there were Frank and his diminutive wife Mimi, both dressed to the nines and bearing a bottle of champagne. By then I'd moved to the kitchen and left the front door ajar for any stragglers.

It was as jolly as I'd remembered it. Caleb presided over the kitchen island, mixing martinis in an old lemonade pitcher and doling them out in glasses of every shape and size to people who bore them off into the hallway, where they stood, backs against the wall, blocking traffic. By the way they chattered, you'd have thought that these people didn't see enough of each other at work, squabbling over the newest news on black holes and high-temperature super- conductors; conducting pitched battles over super symmetry and the theory of everything. Off by the fireplace, Dana: did you see that great new Simpson's cartoon on the Tracey Ullman Show? In the den, Edwin: are you insane? Of course, Ronald Reagan was behind the arms for hostages deal. And, wafting through the house, a complex background smell of chili and smoke spiked with gin and perfume, mixing and merging with the sound of Whitney Houston belting out *I Wanna Dance with Somebody*.

It was interesting going through the whole thing again. I'd remembered my house full of people, jollity and chaos, but the way I see it is that memory is like a fresco, set and hardened into plaster. The elements of composition are all there: line, shape, color, texture. But it lacks the immediacy of the moment, the dynamic feeling that you are there and wielding the brush. Or is the act of creation itself an illusion? Did I paint that picture myself and, if so, could I retouch it now?

Dr. Joliet spilled his drink on the corner of the living room rug. I told him not to worry, that as far as I knew gin didn't stain, but I went into the kitchen anyway to get some water and a paper towel to blot it out, sidling past Henri in front of my bookshelf, who was skimming lightning-fast through Bertrand Russell's *Principia Mathematica*. As I walked into the kitchen, I couldn't help but notice Mimi on the wall phone, in her silk cocktail dress and pearls, long black hair styled into some elaborate up-do, talking intently to what could only be the babysitter. She'd told me early on that this was the first time she'd left the baby with anyone other than Frank or herself, and she was feeling insanely uneasy. Right now was the third time I'd found her on the phone, once in the den and twice in the kitchen. It was hard to believe how we used to be so shackled to land phones.

"Warm the bottle up in the microwave for fifteen seconds," she was saying. "Four ounces, no more. Just test it on your wrist. Make sure it's warm to the touch, but nothing more than that."

Of course, I'd never had a baby, so I couldn't say, but Mimi sounded a little obsessive. Maybe you naturally freak out with your first child, I don't know.

"Give it to her and when she's finished, put her down. Just make sure the clown night light is on. She'll fuss if it isn't…."

As I remember, Frank remarked once or twice about how Mimi had transferred her prodigious management skills to being a mother, and that yes, she sometimes went a little too far.

As I turned from the sink, Caleb stepped in front of me, looking drunk. I tried to duck, but he already had his arm around my shoulders. "You're looking very lovely tonight, Mar-gar-et," he slurred.

"Um, thank you," I said, stepping out from beneath his arm.

"Oh, no you don't," Caleb countered. "I've been waiting all night to talk to you."

"Really?" I said, indicating the paper towel in my hand.

"Well, maybe later. I'm on my way to mop something up in the living room."

"No, not formula, Debbie!" I heard behind me.

"Not later. Now," Caleb insisted, grabbing hold of my arm and twisting me around.

"Caleb, please. You're hurting me," I said, but I couldn't seem to shake him off.

"I just want to talk to you," he slurred.

"First get your hand off of my arm."

"Okey-dokey," Caleb said, removing his hand.

"I made a special point of expressing my milk before I left," Mimi was saying behind me. "It's the little bottle to the left on the top shelf in the refrigerator."

"What is it?" I asked Caleb.

"What is what?"

"You said you wanted to talk to me."

"Oh," Caleb said, thinking hard. "Oh, yes. I find you very attractive, Margaret. Do you...do you want to go upstairs with me?"

I laughed. The guy was sloshed. "Actually, no, Caleb. I don't want to go upstairs with you."

"I could make you very happy," he said, holding onto the island for balance.

"I've got to go, Caleb. But I think you've had a wee bit to drink. Why don't you go lie down somewhere?"

"But that's exactly what I want to do!" He looked at me with a triumphant smile. "With you, of course."

I made a move to leave, but he grabbed me, one hand

around my middle, the other cupping my breast. "Make you very hap-py," he slurred.

"I'll call again in fifteen minutes," Mimi said, hanging up the phone.

Thank God for Frank, who had just now entered the kitchen, calling, "Mimi? Are you still in here?" He took one look at Caleb with his hand on my breast and pulled it off. "Caleb," he said, "you are definitely in need of some black coffee."

"No, Frank, I'm jus' fine," Caleb protested, his arms outstretched to regain their hold on my tits.

"No you're not," Frank said, steering him away from the island and into the living room where coffee was set up. "Be a good boy, Caleb, and have a cup of coffee. Now, would you like some rum cake?" I heard as they went out.

I followed with the wet paper towel.

"Frank," Mimi's voice wafted behind us. "We better go. Debbie can't get the baby to sleep."

That, by the way, signaled a new stage in Caleb's vendetta with Frank and me. I don't think he remembered all that happened, but he came away from the party with a chip on his shoulder and a determination to lord it over me whenever he could. And having Caleb for an enemy was asking for trouble.

Caleb had always shown signs of being a control freak. A couple of years ago, he had volunteered to be advisor for the *Garriston News*, just so he could head off any bad news that might appear about himself. In department meetings, he would shout down any opponents who threatened to get in the way of a pet project or the use of his textbook. He'd bury you with budgetary minutia or attack your credentials, lie, cheat, whatever worked.

I'd hoped that something I could change this time around would temper his resentment against the two of us. I didn't care so much about myself, but I've felt responsible for what happened to Frank for a quarter of a century. If I'd succeeded in tipping that box of Bagel Bites into the shopping cart, maybe I could change something at that party. But no, it was word for word what happened before.

CHAPTER 7

I'M NOT SURE THAT the party reinstated me as a respectable member of the Physics Department, but life went on smoothly for a while after the party. Frank stayed out of my way as much as he could. In department meetings I'd sometimes look up to find him gazing at me dreamily. He'd meet my eyes with a sheepish smile, then just as quickly look away. But he never came up to me if he could help it. The old easy ways before the kiss were gone. It seemed stupid to me then, and just as stupid now. He was acting like a school boy. I almost expected him to sneak up in back of me and pull my pigtails. I could understand his loyalty to his wife and baby, but it just wasn't enough of a reason for me.

So maybe that was the reason 35 took the bull by the horns, and set about seducing him. Though I've reflected countless times on why I became the aggressor in our relationship, I never came to any better conclusion than that I knew he was in love with me, I was with him, and damn his old-fashioned morals, I was going to have him. I'm not proud of this, but it was what it was.

But riding around as I was in what sometimes seemed like someone else's rented body, I was able to be a little more detached this time around. I'd feel everything I felt before, but maybe going through it more than once gives one some perspective. I could see now that the right thing to do was to just let him go. But what could I—60—do about it? It wasn't as if I could physically stop myself from going after him. So, after a going back and forth on who was right and who was wrong and whether any of the responsibility fell on my older self, I gave up the effort and just went along for the ride.

It was one thirty in early June. Most of the undergraduates had taken their last exam and gone home. I was standing, alone, in the front room of my lab, looking out the window, scanning the campus green. In the background played the constant tympani of jackhammers, the earsplitting squeal of electric saws, the last of the construction to renovate the building. I remembered the relief of the last of all this. Who knew I'd be in the midst of it again?

I could make out Frank across the green, a stick figure in tan and white but unmistakably he, striding from his office to lunch. I'd been waiting impatiently for some sign of him since noon. Frank had this tendency to get totally preoccupied in whatever he was doing, whether it was discussing coursework with a student, or losing himself in his research. He'd become enthralled in his work and forget to eat or go home. Predicting when he'd go to lunch, therefore, was a challenge.

High in a skyscraper, though, I was in the position not only to discern his whereabouts but to measure how fast he was walking and where his trajectory was leading him. Leaving right now, I would definitely be able to catch him somewhere in the University Center. I crossed the floor to the front door of the lab, and took the elevator down. Frank was a smudge at the end of the green. I followed him at a leisurely pace to the basement floor, where the old cafeteria stood.

I stood there looking back and forth before I saw him on line, being handed a plate of something brown and white by a fat lady in a hairnet. Funny to see this all again. The last time I was here it was when it opened as the Food Circus, a large donut of food concessions around a central "hole" of tables and chairs, a million dollars in the making but so successful the university all but made up the investment in four years. That would have been 2008, with the last four years pure gravy, so to speak. The students showed their overwhelming preference for a choice between fast food, Chinese food, Italian or vegetarian by voting with their mouths. No one frequented the other dining room on campus.

But here I was back in the old cafeteria with the steamed-up glass counters, the old laminate tables, the bitter tang of burnt pots, overcooked broccoli and fish. It was an experience that, along with the banging and the sawing and the dust in the science building, I had no wish to re-encounter. Nevertheless, I had come for a purpose.

I noticed Frank rolling his tray along the tarnished rails to the cash register. I waited till he had put his change back in his wallet and moved off before I poured myself a cup of weak coffee and followed him to his little corner table.

He was facing the window, his back toward me. I quickly swung around the table, backlit against the glare of the sun.

"Hi," I said, sliding down into the seat across from him.

"Um," is all he could get out, a gob of chicken in his mouth.

I took a sip of dishwater coffee, waiting for Frank to chew and swallow.

"It's ready to go. Again," I said.

"It?" Frank asked, swallowing.

"The time travel experiment," I whispered.

"Ah," he said, putting down his fork, his interest piqued. "What turned out to be the problem?"

"An electrical short. I knew it couldn't have been significant. The concept is sound."

His eyes were looking unusually glittery, or maybe it was the glare of the sun. "I think so, too," he said and picked up his fork again.

He didn't say anything else. I know why but 35 didn't.

"Well, when are we going to try again?" I asked.

Frank put the fork down. His eyes were glittery again. "Margaret, I'd like to help, but you know I can't. Find someone else. One of your grad students."

I could tell from the churning in my stomach that this was not acceptable.

"No!" I said. "I need you, Frank."

He looked at me with those liquid eyes. "Don't try to manipulate me, Margaret."

I tried to stop the next words, but they came out anyway. "If you won't do it, I'll do it alone."

"Oh, for God's sake. Don't do that. You don't know what can go wrong."

"Nothing can go wrong," I said. "Not this time."

"It can, Margaret. It has once already."

I remembered then what I had been thinking the first time we had this conversation. That Frank never copped out on anyone; that once he started something, he always followed through. He was teetering on the edge and all he needed was one good push. "It's important, Frank," I said. "We've got to do this."

We looked at each other, his face in pain, mine in triumph.

"Fine," he sighed. "Tell me when."

We set the date for two days from then.

◊

ON THE WAY BACK across the green, I could hear someone call my name. I turned my head to see a young woman dressed in an acid-green top belted over jean shorts and finished off with hiking boots.

"Dr. Braverman," Janie Carr called again, rushing to catch up with me.

"What can I do for you, Ms. Carr?" I sighed, slowing my pace.

Her denim purse had slipped down her arm, bringing her off-the-shoulder top along with it. As Janie stopped to pull them both up, she reached into her purse. "I just have a few questions for you," she said, pulling out her pen and notebook.

"What now?" I asked, stopping abruptly to face her. I had this reputation for not suffering fools lightly, and I guess this was one of those times.

"Well, for starters, what can you tell me about your project?" Janie asked.

"There's really nothing to tell," I replied, starting to walk again.

"Is time travel possible?" she asked, staying at my side.

"Theoretically," I said.

"Could you tell me how it could be done?"

"Theoretically," I said again. I thought that was quite clever, but it didn't get a rise out of her.

"Would it involve a wormhole like in *Contact*?" she asked, her notebook bobbing up and down as she went along.

Several years before, the astronomer and novelist Carl Sagan had asked the physicist Kip Thorne how to explain a wormhole through space-time. The result was not only a serious scientific description of the phenomenon in Sagan's book *Contact*, but some ground-breaking scientific papers by Thorne about time travel. It was an interesting anecdote but I wasn't going to get into it with her. "Why don't you write Carl Sagan then?" I said, instead.

"I'd rather, Dr. Braverman, that you tell me how *you* did it."

How you *did it*. Didn't I say this young woman was tricky?

"I never said I did any such thing, Ms. Carr. And don't you quote me as saying I did."

"But if you did…."

"If I did, I wouldn't tell you. I never go public with any of my research until I have something to tell. And then it would be in a reputable journal, not our campus newspaper."

"Off the record?" Janie asked.

"Neither on or off the record."

"Dr. Braverman," Janie said, changing tactics. "I'm a senior majoring in journalism. I graduate this year. It's a dog-eat-dog world out there, and I'm going to need a job. This story could get me noticed. This could be my big break." *Please give me something,* she pleaded with heavily shadowed hound dog eyes.

I stopped short, as Janie kept going. When she realized I was several paces behind her, she halted and turned around. "Yes?" she said, hope in her eyes.

As I remember, I was tempted to tell the world, but I knew better. A lot of academics chided me for what they considered loose thinking, and I wasn't going to open myself up to ridicule in front of the whole university. You give license to a youngster at a campus paper, and, believe me, you are asking for whatever you get. "No," I said, resuming my walk.

Janie stood there for a few seconds, reassessing the situation. "Then I'm just going to have to go with what I have!" she called out. I knew then that I had made a mistake.

◊

TWO DAYS LATER, THE backroom door carefully locked behind us, I seated myself in the barber chair. The mechanism was still set for May 3, 5:03 p.m, the time and date when my future self was expected to be seated in the chair.

"You checked the wiring?" Frank asked, for the umpteenth time.

"You know I did," I said, pulling the helmet down over my head and into position.

"If you're ready," he said, laying his hand on the small black button on the back side of the helmet.

"I'm ready!" I cried, impatient.

"Here goes," Frank said, pressing the button.

I had braced myself for the whoosh of disembodiment, for flying off into the void with only my cognition intact, for anything but what actually happened, which was… nothing. Frank looked on, expectant, with no notion of what he should be seeing, and thus, no idea that nothing was happening. It wasn't as if he expected me to physically disappear. It was more that my eyes might go blank for a nanosecond of our time, before my—call it what you will—spirit was back. The trip there, the trip back, and days, months or even years of living inside some deep aneurysm of time would all be hidden from his point of view.

After a half a minute, defeated, I pushed the helmet up.

"You're back?" Frank asked, excited.

"I never left."

"You sure?" he asked, incredulous.

"Yes, I'm sure, dammit."

For the next three hours, we went over every detail of the science, the mechanics of the machine, the theory. We checked the software, the wiring, the interface. We had failed, but nothing seemed to be wrong. I was devastated, as was Frank: all that time and effort wasted. I threw myself across his broad chest and just wept. Frank could do nothing more than stroke the little blonde spikes of hair that had grown back in the past month and a half.

Then, gently, he kissed the top of my head. Then my forehead, then the tears on my cheeks. And finally, as Frank lifted my face from the big wet spot on his oxford shirt, he softly kissed my lips. Then, all of a sudden, as it had happened before, and as I had prayed for it to happen again, we were on the floor, clothes flying, bodies thrashing, all of our entire lives just foreplay for this moment.

◊

FRANK MADE SURE TO leave first. I stuck around, righting the chair we'd overturned, checking for any unmatched earrings or socks hiding in the corners. Probably, I thought, we shouldn't have done that. Sure I wanted him, but I knew what this led to, and that was exactly what I should be trying to stop. Frank had a wife and a baby, and I didn't want to be a home wrecker. At sixty I should have learned how to fight against my natural inclinations.

Yet, in the afterglow of sexual satisfaction, I didn't want to do any such thing. I wanted to give in to all my natural inclinations; to fall into all my old self-destructive patterns, if they made me feel this good. Furthermore, I realized I had a growing feeling of embodiment, as if the ecstasy of sex had mapped every body part to a corresponding piece of my conscious mind. I was no longer a tenant in this body. I was an owner!

With effort, with my hands resting at my sides, I found that I could move not only my right pinky finger but the two adjoining fingers on my right hand, a triumph diminished only by a vague uneasiness, most likely 35 wondering what was causing this spasm in her right hand. By the end of the year, I thought, warming to the topic, with what I hoped would be regular infusions of sex, who knew how much of this thing might I control?

It was now twenty minutes after Frank had left, so I opened up the front door and went out myself. The night was warm; the dormitories dark and campus almost silent. I walked the rest of the way to the parking lot in a mist of quiet contentment, as happy as I would ever be again.

It wasn't until I got into my beloved old 1980 Mustang that I remembered that the experiment had failed, and worse, that neither of us had any idea why. The first time this had happened to me was serious, but it was worse now. If the machine didn't work going into the future, how would I ever get back?

Not, I thought as I started the motor, that there was anything wrong with that.

CHAPTER 8

W E'RE ALL MIND TRAVELERS in our memories.

It must have been in eighty-five, one of many times Frank and I went off after classes to discuss the project. The more we got into it, the less we wanted to risk being seen by anyone in the department, because, frankly, I wasn't supposed to be working on this at all. So, we took separate cars to a no-frills pub in a blue-collar neighborhood a town away. Caesar's was a drafty old space the size of the warehouse it used to be, with windows high along one wall and no windows at all around the other three. A long polished bar took up the whole length of one side, mirrors in back reflecting an endless row of bottles. A vast signboard above the bar listed pizzas, subs and cheese steaks, along with fries, onion rings and half a dozen decadent desserts. Hey, no one was there to eat health food.

It was a weekday night happy hour, and the place was hopping as it usually was: guys in plaid flannel shirts, jeans and hardhats; young women in scrubs and candy stripes; paunchy workmen, their plumber's cleavage hanging out in back; a smattering of an older crowd. We didn't know a soul, and that was good.

Some fifty-odd identical laminate tables lined up in half a dozen cockeyed rows, broken every hundred feet or so by bearing columns, relics of the building's industrial past. There weren't a lot of tables left. I parked myself at the last one on the window-side while Frank got us two Miller drafts from the bar. A bunch of guys at the next table, their tool belts slung over the backs of their chairs, were laughing and whooping it up, a dozen empties down, another round or three to go.

Frank deposited our two mugs on the table and sat down. He looked tired but happy to be here. We had tried to get together the Tuesday before, and the Tuesday before that, but work and prior engagements had conspired against us.

"To time travel," I toasted, raising my glass in the air. So did a hunky guy at the next table, looking meaningfully at me. I couldn't help but chuckle. With all the ruckus, I figured he hadn't heard what he was drinking to.

"To time travel," Frank agreed, raising his glass with a smile.

As yet there was no machine, just a handful of high-flying ideas and a penciled sketch on graph paper, grounded in the basic principles we had already discussed. We hadn't finalized who would be the passenger, though from the beginning I insisted it had to be me, since it was my idea in the first place. We hadn't even talked about where I'd be going.

"The future or the past?" I asked him now, over the racket from the next table.

"The future," Frank said without hesitation. "You can't go back."

I put my beer down. "I don't see why not. Physics doesn't forbid time going backwards. Anyway, I've always wanted to go back to save my dog Frisky."

Frank looked at me quizzically, so I told him the whole sad story of how I came home late to find Frisky floating belly-up in the pool, and how the whole thing was my fault. That led us into a long discussion of pets, whether cats or dogs or for that matter dolphins or octopi are the smartest, why I was insisting that I should be the guinea pig, the first time each of us got drunk, free will, all of this reverting in roundabout fashion to why one can't go back in time. By now I had bought another round, and we were well on our way to finishing that one.

"Theoretically," Frank was saying, "backwards time isn't forbidden, but it hasn't been demonstrated either. The whole issue was mainly a thought experiment, anyway. I'm not sure it can be proven at all."

"Not even by you?" I asked coyly, thinking that if I handed Frank a marker, he might just dash off the definitive proof on a napkin or a brown paper bag.

He gave me a sideways grin. "Not even by me, Margaret. Besides, as I'm sure you are aware, there are the paradoxes…"

"Ahh, the paradoxes," I said. I raised my glass. "To paradoxes," I toasted. The guy at the next table raised his, too.

Of course, I knew just what Frank had been talking about. They were paradoxes resulting from time travel, in which an individual travels back in time and performs actions that would ultimately have made the time travel impossible in the first place.

"Maybe we should go," Frank said suddenly, peering into my happy, bleary eyes. "I think you've probably had enough."

I looked at my watch: seven o'clock. Not so late. Anyway, time was relative. "You were saying," I prompted.

"Well, it's up to you. I just don't want you to get too sloshed."

"The paradoxes," I reminded him.

He shrugged and went on. "Well, the most well-known one is the grandfather paradox, where the time traveler goes back in time and attempts to kill his grandfather at a time, say, before his grandfather has met his grandmother. If he does so, then his mother or father will never be born and neither will the time traveler himself...."

"In which case," I finished, "the time traveler never would have gone back in time to kill his grandfather in the first place." I laughed and emptied my glass. "One more round?" I asked, gesturing to Frank's empty glass.

"You've really had enough, Margaret...."

I leaned over and laid my hand on Frank's upper arm. He had his sleeves rolled up. I moved my hand down from his sleeve, over a surprisingly hairy forearm, onto his hand. It was a nice hand: strong and square and virile. I kept mine there for a few seconds before I stood up. "My treat," I said.

"No, mine. You got the last one," Frank said, standing up and making his way to the bar.

"Make mine Jack Daniels on the rocks this time," I called after him. Frank was probably right. I had probably had enough, but I'd never let that stop me before.

By accident I caught the eye of that same hunk at the next table, who leered at me for a minute or so until I looked away. He was a good-looking guy with dark shiny hair and macho Don Johnson stubble, but he just wasn't my type. Probably all balls and no brain....Not that there was anything wrong with that.

Just that I wanted someone tall and serious, profound, gallant, geekily funny, someone like, like—Frank! Thinking back now, I realize I was already half in love with him. I don't think he was yet in love with me, but I wanted him to be.

I watched as Frank wended his way back, two serious-looking drinks in his hands. "Last round," he said, setting my Jack Daniels in front of me.

I took a long drink. "So," I said.

"So," he said, his blue eyes locking onto mine.

We laughed, for no particular reason.

"I can't go back," I said.

"No, you can never go back," Frank agreed.

We laughed again, madly. Then we sat there for a minute or so looking intimately into each other's eyes.

All of a sudden Frank broke the silence with, "And then there was the one about the art critic from the future who visits Leonardo da Vinci."

"Is this a joke?" I asked, ready to laugh at anything.

"No, a paradox. Now, seeing da Vinci's current work, the critic finds it mediocre and concludes that the artist has yet to produce his great paintings. To encourage him, he gives the painter a reproduction of his painting of the woman with the famous smile. Unbeknownst to the critic, however, Leonardo sets about meticulously copying the reproduction onto canvas….And voilà, the Mona Lisa!"

"So the painting came out of nowhere," I said, laughing.

"The knowledge paradox, they call it." Frank grinned. "The reproductions exist because they are copied from the paintings, and the paintings exist because they're copied from the reproductions."

"I love it," I said, taking a slug of Jack Daniels. "But, anyway, the paradoxes don't apply in my case. I wouldn't be going back in body or bringing anything material with me."

"Margaret," Frank said, all of a sudden serious. "It's not about physical matter. It's about the prospect of changing the future."

Of course, now I realize that this was the very point of his objection. Paradoxes are not just funny jokes. They're warnings. Actions have consequences. Screw around in the past and you may not be here to screw around. Don't expect to get something for nothing. You might just get nothing for something. But at 33, somewhat drunk and in love, with my whole life ahead of me, I thought I could do anything I wanted, and nothing bad would happen. And as for the universe, it could surely take care of itself. So, I blew off his objection with the first rebuttal I could think of.

"Well, if that's the concern," I said, "there's always Novikov's self-consistency conjecture."

In the mid-eighties, an Igor Dmitrievich Novikov, Professor of Astrophysics at Copenhagen University, came out with a theory that, in the course of backwards time travel any attempt to cause a paradox would fail. If you tried to kill your grandfather years before your birth, something would prevent it from happening. Your dog would distract you; your gun would jam, or your car would break down. One way or another, any change endangering the self-consistency of the past had to fail.

"True," Frank said. "That would make it impossible to create time paradoxes in the first place. But it's only a conjecture after all."

We finished our drinks in thoughtful silence.

"So, in the last analysis," I said, finally, "either I can go back or I can't. If the past is fixed, the universe will just refuse to let me travel backwards in time."

"Or it will let you go," Frank countered, "but you won't be able to change anything."

"Or it will let me go, and I *will* be able to change the past. But, accidentally stepping on an ant, I'll extinguish all life on earth."

Frank, chuckling, took my hands in his. "Now, you wouldn't want that, would you, Margie?"

The nickname made me start a little. He'd never called

me anything other than Margaret before. He'd also never taken my hands in his. I didn't want to do anything that would ruin the moment.

"No," I agreed. "I think I better just go forwards."

◊

IT'S ONE THING TO revisit an event in one's memory. It's another to see it there in all its glory before you. To look out the window onto my backyard in June of 1987, as I was just now, and to behold it as it was twenty-five years ago. Now, that was a miracle.

My little yard never looked so good: the grass a vibrant green; the rhododendrons in full bloom. The marigolds and pansies and begonias I'd purchased at the local nursery still with their original complement of flowers I'd bought them with: everything in its prime and at its peak.

I always had my parents out for Father's Day. After that, I'd inevitably lose my motivation to water, the flowers would dry up and drop off, the grass would turn to straw, and the whole gestalt would fall apart.

Sometimes I'd wonder why I'd never been able to change my ways. Every spring I'd start out with such high hopes and every fall I'd end up with the same unholy mess. Be that as it may, this is why it was so important to have the two of them over before the backyard crumbled to dust.

They'd come out by train from the City, where they had lived forever: first in Brooklyn, then in Queens, then in the holy grail of Manhattan, where they resided in a nice old doorman building on the West Side. They liked it there.

My father had his terrace with its wide-open view of the Hudson, at least until all those new high-rises went up and blocked it out. My mother would stand on line at 42nd Street to pick up half-price theater tickets, some of them stinkers, of course, but triumphing now and then with tickets to Guys and Dolls with Nathan Lane for ("would you believe it?" she'd say) ten dollars apiece.

I can't think of them without a lump in my throat and tears coming to my eyes. They were good people—with their faults of course—Dad had a temper and Mom could be a space cadet—but good, good people—and Dad's been gone for almost twenty years; Mom for close to ten. Theirs is no different from any of the other stories, I guess: one tale in a city with eight million, but it's theirs alone, and it's been over for some time now.

So, it's a wondrous thing that they are coming again for Father's Day. We'll say the same things we said before. Mom will bring me a bathing suit she bought for herself but neglected to try on and now realizes it is way too young for her but would look perfect on you, dear. Dad will go to plant the marigolds I left on the lawn because I never got to them, but will see fit to advise me that the soil is poor and let's go to the nursery to get a couple of bags of peat moss first. We'll take a walk to town and buy the pickles I forgot and have a deli lunch on the patio. Same old, same old, but that's just the point. To see them again! To hug! To talk! To laugh! Priceless, as they say.

Mom carries out the plates of corned beef, tongue and

turkey, and I bring out the condiments, the rye bread and the beer. We eat on paper plates and drink straight from the bottles. "Passion food," Dad says, nodding knowingly at Mom, as he pops a fat Kalamata olive into his mouth. She gives him a shy smile I never noticed before. No doubt this is some sexual allusion, but 35 doesn't notice, busy thinking of something else, I guess, the way I always used to be with the two of them: there in body but not in mind. I remember now, and I regret it. I resolve today, if all I can be is mind, at least to be there fully.

We each make our own sandwiches: Mom, her usual mix of tongue and turkey, a little mayonnaise, a little ketchup, a leaf of lettuce, a shred of tomato; and Dad, a more impulsive amalgamation of every meat on the table, slathered with mustard, pickle, onion, tomato. Hold the lettuce. I have long since given up red meat, but find myself smearing brown mustard on fresh bread and heaping corned beef between the slices until my hands can hardly fit around it. Well, if I can't change anything, I might as well enjoy it, I decide. The first mouthful of salty, tangy, fatty, meaty, juicy beef, the sour chewiness of the bread, the zippy bite of mustard, all mixed up together, a whole so over and above the sum of its parts, it all but blows me away.

The house was constructed west to east on the lot, so that the front door faces the driveway, which is, of course, perpendicular to the street. That means the house is aligned sideways on the property, with no backyard to speak of, but a large side yard to the east, all edged in overgrown bushes that keep my privacy. So by noon the yard is always in full sunshine. I hoist the umbrella above the outdoor table and we sit, our backs to the sun, and savor our sandwiches and sip our beer.

The warmth of the sun and the beer, the magic of the company, and the sweet serenity of one insignificant lazy afternoon is something I do not remember. But this time around it seems to sum up all the things I missed. Too hardworking to take an afternoon off, too ambitious to value doing nothing for its own sake, sure that the three of us had all the time in the world twenty-five years ago, I took this afternoon for granted. This time I know not to.

"Your new haircut is very pretty," my mother says, putting down her sandwich.

I know she means that the burnt parts have all been cut off and styled into something that looks almost deliberate. "Thanks," I say. "I found a local woman who does a nice job."

"I certainly hope you got rid of that hazardous hair dryer," Mom says.

I have, of course, told her nothing of the explosion, the experiment, or my public chastisement. As far as she knows, my hair dryer malfunctioned. My philosophy was always to tell them only what they needed to know; otherwise, they worried. They knew I taught physics at Garriston University, and that was about it. They never asked a lot of questions about my research, because they were certain they wouldn't understand it. But would they have been shocked to find out I was experimenting with time travel? You betcha. That I had a married lover? Yup. And would I ever in my wildest dreams have hinted at any of this? No way.

All of a sudden, though, I have the strongest urge to tell them the truth. I want to establish a bond instead of shrugging them off, because you never realize what you have until you lose it. If I possibly can, I decide, I will tell them everything: how I tried for years to travel in time but failed until now. That I have come back from the future just so that I can do things better this time, and that this is one of those times. I concentrate as hard as I can on opening my mouth and forming the words for all this. I try intently for several minutes, but can establish no connection between my mind to the motor cortex in this brain, nor can I find any path from there to the muscle fibers of the mouth. Not only can I not utter a thing, but I cannot even signal the brain to stop eating the scrumptious chocolate chip coffee cake I have just brought out. All I manage to do, after the mouth leisurely finishes up its eating, and when, with excruciatingly slowness, the hands complete their wiping of the mouth with a napkin, is to ease the right hand several inches over to cover Mom's hand with my own and to squeeze the slightest little bit.

CHAPTER 9

THE FOLLOWING WEEK AT two o'clock, one of my undergrads was leaving my office, having just persuaded me to up his grade from C+ to B- on the last exam, and Caleb was on his way in. As usual, he just barged in, pushing the student back against the door frame. Then as the young man left, Caleb closed the door, turning the sign on the door from "Come in" to "Back tomorrow," and dropped into the chair facing me.

There are two chairs in my office: one for me, and one for the rare visitor. Behind the battered desk stands a single precarious bookshelf crammed with physics books I haven't looked at in years. Along the adjacent wall lies a lone window so dirty I have to dredge my memory to recall what it looks out upon. The room is an eyesore. No one comes to this office for a social call except Caleb, and I wish he wouldn't.

"My office hours go till three," I protested.

"Don't worry your little head about it," he said, easing himself back into the chair.

"Caleb, you are so patronizing," I told him.

"You feminists have no sense of humor, you know that?" Caleb shot back, his fat face looking genuinely hurt.

"One, I'm not a feminist. And two, your so-called jokes aren't funny. They're insulting."

"That's my point. You women are just too sensitive."

"Like your 'joke' the other day," I continued, ignoring his comment, "about the gene for intelligence being based on the Y chromosome. Not funny."

"Everyone else laughed," Caleb said, crossing his legs.

"Not everyone, and, besides, all the other people in the room were men."

"Could be the gene for humor is also on the Y chromosome," Caleb quipped.

"Damn it, Caleb," I said, standing up. I never could figure the guy out. Half a dozen times he insinuates how much he'd like to get me in bed, but then he goes and insults my intelligence. Some people are clueless.

"Anyway," Caleb chuckled. "That's not what I came here to talk about."

"Okay," I said, sitting back down. "What is it?"

"Janie Carr called me this morning."

I felt a jolt of adrenalin, but 35 played it cool. "Did she now?" I said.

"She says that she saw a man coming out of your lab last night. Must have been around nine."

Another jolt of adrenalin, this time stronger. "What's she doing, spying on me?"

"No law against standing in the hallway of the science building," Caleb said with a grin. "The thing is, you didn't come out for another twenty minutes."

"Jesus, Caleb. Why are you even talking to her?"

"Hey, she says you won't talk to her. She pleaded with

you, she says, to tell her something—anything—but you said no."

"I don't have to give out information on my research until I'm good and ready."

"Well, that's why she came to me. I'm advisor to the paper, you'll remember," Caleb said. "Anyway, who's the man? Janie didn't know. Just said he's tall. Could it be... Frank?"

"I don't have to account to you for anything," I said, folding my arms across my chest.

"Well aren't we defensive," clasping his hands behind his head and leaning back. "I wonder what you're hiding."

I remembered the gist of this conversation, not the details, so I couldn't have helped 35 even if I wanted to. "Nothing," I said.

"Well, Janie said he looked a little disheveled when he came out."

I made a dismissive face. "In that case, it could be anyone in the department except Henri D'Amboise."

"The way Janie sees it," Caleb went on, letting that one pass, "is either the two of you were having a roll in the hay, or you were having another go at that time machine of yours."

Right on, I couldn't help thinking. Both of the above. But 35 was giving him nothing. "Neither. And, next time you see Janie Carr, I'd appreciate it if you asked her to stop snooping around. If there's something I want her to know, I'll call her."

"Well, that's just what Janie wants you to do. She told me to tell you that she's at the *Garriston News* office most afternoons and evenings and to call anytime. By the way, Margaret," Caleb said, looking at me sideways, "I like the way your hair is growing in. It looks—I don't know— Audrey Hepburn-ish. It fits your face."

I could see a shadow through the glass in my door. The shadow looked like it was reading something, like a sign. "Come in!" I called out. Nothing happened. "I'm in!" I cried.

The door cracked open and a pretty young head peeked through. "I don't want to interrupt anything," the girl said, looking at the two of us.

"Oh, Dr. Winter's just leaving, Tammy," I said, waving her in.

"It's about the last exam," she said easing into the room. She had on a short, tight skirt and a form-fitting sweater that Caleb couldn't quite take his eyes off of.

"Dr. Winter," I said. "I'm afraid we'll have to discuss that matter at another time."

Caleb stood up and gallantly gave up his chair, his eyes on the sweater all the way out.

◊

I PICKED UP THE TOP newspaper from a stack of *Garriston News* that materialized every Tuesday afternoon at one in the lobby of the science building. There, in bold print was the lead story: **"Time-Travel Experiment Denied by Physics Professor."**

35 went white, but, of course I'd known all along that Janie would twist a denial into something newsworthy. I folded the paper and carried it upstairs into the privacy of my lab before I sat down and began to read.

> At 9:15 on the night of June 4th, a tall disheveled male figure was seen coming out of Dr. Margaret Braverman's lab. Twenty minutes later, the light in the lab went out and Dr. Braverman herself followed, somewhat rumpled herself, locking the door behind her. It is no crime to work late, but what were they doing in there? Why were they so disheveled? And who was the tall man?
>
> It's been rumored that there is a time machine in the backroom of the Braverman lab, and that the explosion on May 3 which sent Dr. Braverman to the hospital, was the result of something that went dreadfully wrong. Only pulling out the plug by a likely assistant, in a desperate attempt to halt the experiment seems to have saved her. Could this tall man be the professor's mystery assistant?
>
> Dr. Braverman, whose hair was scorched and whose skin was burnt,

has since recovered, but, when approached recently by this reporter, would only say that time travel was "theoretically" possible. Dr. Braverman denied that she had done an experiment in time travel at all. However, in response to a question of how she did it, she confessed,

"If I did, I wouldn't tell you. I never go public with any of my research until I have something to tell. And then it would be in a reputable journal, not our campus newspaper."

35 went white at this, too. Of course, I remembered what I'd done the first time around, but there was nothing I could do to stop myself from doing it all over again. So, I called the newspaper to get it to publish a retraction and/ or to collect the stacks of newly printed papers, but some youngster with a voice that hadn't changed yet told me he was the only one there. He'd tell his editor, he said. What was his name, I asked. "Jerry Monahan," he said. I gave Jerry Monahan my name and number, but nothing much materialized. When the editor, who didn't sound much older, called back later that day, he asked whether I had been misquoted. I said it wasn't the quotes so much as the lurid and misleading tone of the story. He said it seemed awfully mild to him, but that he'd reread it and get back to

me. As I remember, last time around he never did. And by a week from now I would have new problems, so if the past is any indication, I'd let the whole thing drop.

But it wasn't over just yet. The following morning I got a call in my office.

"Margaret," a worried voice said.

"Hello mystery assistant," I replied. Just hearing his voice made my heart jump, but 35 acted cool. "I haven't heard from you in two weeks, so I guess this is about the article."

There was a long gulp at the other end. I figured it was Frank's usual Dunkin' Donuts extra-large coffee with cream, a morning habit he'd had as long as I knew him. "How did this happen?" he asked finally. "I thought you weren't talking to the campus newspaper."

"Janie Carr cornered me on campus," I confessed. "But I didn't tell her anything."

"Apparently, you did."

"I promise you, Frank, I didn't say anything. Caleb told me…"

"What's Caleb doing in this?"

I sighed. "She's going to him because I won't talk to her. Anyway, Caleb says that Janie was there waiting in the hallway outside my lab and saw both of us coming out that night."

"Waiting in the hallway?! So she saw me. Why didn't she print who it was?"

"I guess she didn't recognize you. Thank God for small blessings."

"Does Caleb know?"

"He surmised, but nothing certain."

There was a minute of silence, slurping in the background. Finally, Frank told me the reason he had called.

"I hadn't even seen the article. But I had this week's *Garriston News* among some papers I brought home. Mimi read it before I did," he said. "She told me she's been looking forward to the next installment of the 'mysterious accident in the physics lab.'" I could hear another gulp on the other end. "This morning she asked me whether I knew who Margaret's 'mysterious partner' was."

I almost choked. "I don't suppose you told her."

"I told her I had no idea."

For a long time, Mimi was almost a complete unknown to me. From the little I'd heard, she sounded difficult to live with, and Frank had mentioned once how jealous she could be. I, on the other hand, seemed more his type. I sometimes wondered why he had married her, but I never got up enough courage to ask "Frank?" I said at last.

"Yes?"

"What would happen if you told her?"

"She'd kill me, that's what."

Maybe that would be a good thing, I thought. Assuming he didn't mean that literally. Maybe that would give the two of us a chance. I knew how hard it would be for him, what with his daughter being so young, but that I loved him and would see him through it. That sometimes when you make a mistake, you can't salvage it. You have to start anew. Two times I almost said this. And two times I chickened out.

◊

WALTER, AS HE ALWAYS did, organized one last department lunch at D'Amato's for the end of the year. We gathered in the parking lot, a small group. Dana had called in that morning to say her son was ill. Dr. Joliet said he was indisposed. Henri was off somewhere doing a presentation for the Rose Planetarium. Edwin begged off, saying he was busy organizing a campaign in support of the National Acid Rain Control Act. So, it was just Walter, Mark, Frank, Caleb, and me.

Five people couldn't quite make it into Walter's Ford Taurus, so we had to split up. Mark offered to take anyone who wanted in the tomato-red Mazda RX-7 turbo he was so proud of. I could see Caleb already sitting in the passenger's seat of the Taurus, so I told Mark I'd take him up on his offer. Frank, who had been headed towards the Mazda, stopped short when he saw me get in, hesitated, then turned on his heel and got into the back seat of the Taurus.

That left Mark and me alone. I couldn't help but notice that he had big blue shadows under those long-lashed dark eyes of his, as if he hadn't slept for a week. He gave me a bright smile as if nothing was wrong, but it didn't cover up the fact that something was. It looked as if Mark needed a good shoulder to cry on, but he never had been one to tell me his problems.

The Mazda was a sleek and sexy sports car, all power and shine and style. Mark revved the motor for my benefit, as he filled me in on its turbocharged rotary engine, its rear-wheel drive, its five-speed manual transmission.

"I myself would have gone for something a little less show-off-y, but Jerry said, "You only live once, you know." He patted the leather dashboard with affection. "Ah, well, he's right."

He's wrong, I thought, but 35 was already agreeing with him.

"D'Amato's, then," Mark said, throwing the car into gear and roaring off, leaving Walter and the rest of the crew in our dust.

We followed most of the same streets the four of us had traveled not so long ago, a quarter of a century in the future. Trenton was, well, different. A few of the old warehouses, empty shells the last I looked, were still in use, their windows small and dirty but neither broken nor boarded up. The city had been in decline ever since the sixties' riots, and still a mess back in 1987, just as it would be twenty-five years later.

Some impressive buildings were on their way up, though. I had forgotten how back then the mayor had been on a tear to build the city up again, to bring the working people back and put up new office space. We passed the new Department of Motor Vehicles, the future television station and a couple of towering steel birdcages, all in the process of going up. Well, the mayor's plan didn't work.

The city never did come back to what it used to be in the fifties, though you can't say he didn't try. Actually, it looked better than I had remembered it.

"I need a sympathetic ear," Mark said all of a sudden, still looking straight ahead.

"Sure," I said.

"It's something I can't tell the guys," he added, giving me a quick look.

I could tell from his eyes that this was not a request for fashion advice. It was dead serious. And, anyway, I knew what was coming.

"Jerry's been fooling around," he said, turning back to the road. "He hasn't told me any of this, of course. He's just always out. All he does is tell me lies, like he's working late, or he's seeing his mother, that sort of thing, but I know he's out in some club picking up some guy. Sometimes he doesn't come home at all."

I remembered figuring Mark must be pretty hard up to be confiding in me, but I guessed there was no one else to tell. His parents, as I remembered, had more or less disowned him.

"I don't suppose you got it wrong. That he really is seeing his mother…?"

A sigh. "I called his mother. She hasn't heard from him in a year."

We drove a couple of minutes in silence.

"I imagine he doesn't want to hurt you," I remarked, not knowing what else to say.

"Whose side are you on?" Mark asked, only half in jest.

"Yours, of course, Mark." The fact is I never liked Jerry much. Too ripped. Pecs and delts and biceps galore, all busting out from under a skin-tight black shirt with the sleeves torn off. Gorgeous, if you like that sort of thing, but really, what was under all that flash?

"If only he were honest with me…." Mark was saying.

"You're right," I told him, more decisively. "A relationship needs to be based on truth."

We passed what used to be the old wire factory; later to be the site of a thriving farmer's market; but at this moment only a pile of burned bricks on an empty lot. Creation, destruction, rebirth, the empty lot seemed to say. Round and round and round. I wondered what it all meant.

"I don't know whether I should confront him," Mark was saying when I roused myself. "If I do, he may just leave."

I had no idea how to answer this. After all, I wasn't exactly the exemplar of lasting relationships. Love was something I hardly understood myself. Physics was easy, love was hard. "How long have the two of you been together?" I asked.

"We just met last year. At a club in the Village. It was a place that catered to mostly white, middle-class, educated gays. I guess I thought it was safe to go to a place like that. Or safer, anyway. Guys who knew enough to wear a condom at least." A little smile grew on his lips, but faded.

"Anyway that's where we met," he went on. "There was a

circular bar, two flights above the street, and a small lounge up another small flight of stairs. A dozen or so small cocktail tables, a pool table and a parquet-tiled open area for dancing and drag shows. He had a pool cue in one hand, a martini in the other. He was laughing at something when our eyes met...."

That was it. He'd give this salacious intro, and then quit. It was classic Mark, but I didn't know that then. He was pretty uptight for a gay man.

"You moved in together?" I prompted.

"Yeah, within the month. He was the one for me. I never gave it another thought." Mark paused. "But apparently he did."

We turned a corner onto Houston to find lights on in the warehouse across the street, the once padlocked barber shop full of customers, and an old Italian market I had almost forgotten existed, with its doors wide open and its rafters ripe with salamis. The street was packed with parked cars, as it always was. Mark drove to the corner and parked a few spots down.

"So you love him?" I asked after he had cut the motor.

"With all my heart," Mark said, wiping at his eye with his sleeve.

Whatever I thought of Jerry didn't matter. It's what Mark thought of him that counted. Love might be mysterious, but I knew at least that if you're lucky to find it, you're an idiot to throw it away.

"Have it out with him, then," I told him. "If you love

Jerry and want to stay together, you may first have to risk his leaving."

Mark gave me a chaste kiss on my cheek. "Thanks," he said. "I guess I needed that."

It really wasn't until we left the car that I realized maybe I should take my own advice.

The wait wasn't as bad as I had remembered: just two couples in front of us, lounging on the steps. Probably a few more inside, stuffed inside the minuscule waiting room, but not too bad. Mark and I stood there, waiting, till the others came. I thought he might resume the conversation, but he didn't.

The first I saw of the other three was Caleb coming towards us, hefting an insulated bag over his shoulder. The bag turned out to be stuffed full of Yuengling beer. He put it down on the sidewalk for the ten minutes it took till it was our turn to squeeze inside the restaurant; then, no surprise, we waited twenty minutes more. The entry way, due to the scorching oven, was hotter than the outside. I had forgotten that the rattling air conditioner D'Amato's owned in 2012 was their lone concession to comfort, and they didn't even give in to that till the late nineties.

Still, the place was packed. Up in the same corner of the room, where the wall met the ceiling, was a small black and white television set tuned, as always, to a Phillies game. No sound, of course. Everything the same, except that in those days baseball was still played in the afternoon, so lunch, not dinner, was the time to watch. Mike Schmidt, one of their star players of the eighties, was up to bat in the old Veterans Stadium.

As I remember, Veterans was built in a circular shape in order to accommodate both football and baseball. It turned out not to be very good for either. They imploded it in 2004, and now it's a parking lot. Citizen's Bank Park is the new one—bigger, better, with all the bells and whistles. Me, I have great affection for Veterans Stadium, whistles or not, so it was neat to see afternoon ball in the old place.

There. Schmidt, swinging hard, just got a double. It occurred to me that I must have seen this very same game twenty-five years ago, the last time we came. I don't remember the outcome, but it's clear it's an exact replay, no different from watching an old movie that doesn't change from one playing to the next. So far nothing had changed in my life this time around either. Mark made his confession to me, just as he had before and just as it would most certainly be followed some years later with the news that Jerry was HIV-positive. What would it take to make things different?

We were five people in a sea of four-seater booths. The only place we could all fit was the single large table to the side of the oven, but at the moment that was filled with a large noisy family lollygagging over the remains of their three pies. Caleb, as was his wont, sauntered over and just stood there, the bag of beer digging into his shoulder. Every time one of them turned around, he gave them a big sigh of *weltschmerz*. Oy, he might have been saying.

MLECTION

The world is such a cruel place where some people take more than their share, while others have to shoulder heavy cases of beer and never get to rest their weary feet. Before long, the squatters had boxed up their pizza, gathered their children, and skedaddled. The table was still full of dishes and crumbs, but Caleb had already leaned over the front counter to demand a clean-up. I had to give him credit; Caleb never let propriety stand in his way in getting what he wanted.

"Sure," said Sal, in the midst of hurling a discus of dough high in the air. His hair was white even then, but he was still barrel-chested and strong. In his later years, he'd continue to go up and down the aisles socializing with the customers, asking them about their children, telling them the same old stories, but by then he'd become fragile with age.

"Angie," he called out, "you want to take care of these customers?"

Angie, at the cash, turned around, smiling, of all things. "Sure, Pop," she said, no attitude in her tone at all. She must have been thirty-something at the time, fresh-faced and pleasant, a little plump but nothing like the broad-beamed battleship she would yet turn out to be. Angela must have worked in this crummy little pizzeria all the years of her life, and I can understand how that might feel like purgatory. But I think it must have been the last twenty-five that turned her against the world.

We watched as Angie came down off her perch at the

register to wipe down the table and lay out five place settings. "What'll youse have?" she asked us when she was done. I would have laughed if I could. Some things never change.

We ordered three pies for the five of us—one plain, one pepperoni, and one red clam—since they cost only eight dollars apiece, and Walter said Mark looked so skinny he could probably use a whole one to himself. Then we sat and waited.

I took the time to look around me. The Formica on our table was undoubtedly the very same material as the familiar stuff with the blur in the center, but without the blur; the knotty pine paneled walls identical, but a little less distressed. Frank Sinatra and Frankie Valli still posed with a young Salvatore D'Amato, but Anthony Scalia, shaking hands with Sal as he looked today, was the last picture in the row. I did a quick calculation. Samuel Alito, born around 1950, would have been 37 at that very moment and probably still Deputy Assistant to Attorney General Ed Meese, nowhere near to being confirmed Supreme Court Justice or being immortalized on D'Amato's rogue's gallery. And, whether there was or was not a Zagat at that time, there was no evidence of it on their walls. D'Amato's back then was strictly a local establishment.

Mark and I sat on the inside, Frank and Walter on the outside, with Caleb holding court at one end. Global warming had for some reason become the table topic, probably because we were seated within half a dozen feet of the blazing hot wood-fired brick oven in a small enclosure with no air-conditioning.

"I think it's obvious that there's a trend toward warming," Walter was saying as he mopped his brow. "Just in this decade it's a fact that the global annual mean temperature curve is rising."

"Walter, if you take the long-range view, I believe you'll find that it's all part of a cycle of natural variations," Caleb countered.

I watched as Sal threw the dough in a high arc and caught it handily with his knuckles. Now he was juggling the pie, throwing it up an imperceptible bit and catching it, throwing it and catching it, each time stretching the dough a little more into a thin, elastic round.

"C'mon, if we continue on this curve, by the next century we'll approach the average temperature of the age of the dinosaurs," Walter was saying. "You call that natural variation?"

I turned back to the table to find Frank, with a faintly bemused smile and his deep blue eyes focused on my face. And suddenly, nothing else—no vigorous debate on climate, no pies soaring acrobatically into the air, no thoughts of the future or the past—could possibly hold my interest.

"You're missing the point, Walter," Caleb was saying, though I hardly heard him. "From the 1940's to the 1970's the global annual temperature was downwards. There were scientists claiming that a new ice age was near. Moreover, ocean sediment research shows that there have been no less than thirty-two cold-warm cycles in the last 2.5 million years. All these ups and downs are just noise."

Noise is what I would have said they were doing. Each of them was going so hot and heavy on the topic that neither noticed that Frank and I were otherwise engaged. It didn't matter at that moment whether the earth was on fire. We had the hots for each other, all without global warming.

"Hansen's already done a paper on that," Walter insisted. "He estimated the noise level of natural climate variability by comparing the predicted warming to the standard deviation of the observed global temperature trend of the past century...."

"A century is way too short a period to base global statistical estimates on," Caleb sneered.

I dropped my napkin accidentally on purpose and went rooting around for it under the table. And who should I meet there but Frank, who had coincidentally dropped a spoon.

"Hi," he said, reaching over for his spoon and accidentally on purpose touching my hand.

"Hi," I whispered. "We've got to stop meeting like this."

Frank pulled me further down, till the two of us were on our knees in the sweet spot between all the legs, and kissed me, lingering a little, savoring the danger of it. Then we both resurfaced with silly smiles on our faces.

"I agree," Mark was saying as the two of us popped up on either side of the table. "We know so little about climate. You know how many variables are involved? Any model would have to take into consideration....solar luminosity, volcanic activity, not to mention human influences...." He broke off, glancing first at Frank, then at me.

"That's the whole point of this, isn't it?" Frank broke in, just to be part of the conversation. "First you have to establish whether there's global warming, but then you have to determine whether it's human caused."

"True," Mark replied, a conspiratorial smile coming to his lips. "If it's a natural occurrence, there's more likelihood it will right itself. If it's human-caused, it's up to us to STOP SCREWING AROUND."

Frank settled himself in his seat, looking abashed, but I wasn't too worried. Mark seemed in better spirits all of a sudden. It could be that I was privy to his secrets, and now he was privy to mine. Checks and balances; that way neither one of us was likely to tell on the other. Or maybe he was just happy for me.

"And Hansen predicts," Walter went on, oblivious, "that CO_2 warming rises beyond one standard deviation noise level in the 1980s and two standard deviations in the 1990s..."

"Again, I say that he's starting with anomalous data," Caleb countered.

"...Proving that CO_2 warming rises above the noise level of natural climate variability in this century," Walter concluded triumphantly.

By this point the pies had come, and no one was listening to him anyway, certainly not Frank or me, not Mark, who had grabbed the first blazing hot slice, not Caleb who never really listened to him in the first place. A second helping of Yuengling came out of the bag, and we all stuffed our faces in high spirits—Walter, because he thought he had won the argument; Caleb because he thought he had; Mark because he was tickled at the novel idea of Frank and Margaret in love; and, last of all, Frank and myself, because we were.

CHAPTER 10

IT WAS THE LAST Physics Department meeting of the school year. Monday morning meeting—M^3—was what we used to call it. The room was warm, even though we'd pulled the shades dowhn to block out the blazing sun. We'd poured our coffee and selected our donuts. Old business had been already been discussed and voted upon. Several of us were beginning to yawn.

All the usual suspects were there. Besides me, there were Dr. Joliet, Erwin, Frank, Caleb, Dana, Walter, Mark, and whatever instructors were passing through in 1987—fewer than in 2012, when the university, in the unenviable place of making up for state funds that had suddenly evaporated, began replacing tenured positions with cheap, expendable adjunct instructors.

The only one missing was Henri D'Amboise, who was busy flying around the country as usual doing presentations and Public Television specials. This wasn't the first M^3 that he'd missed, but you couldn't blame him much. He was in the midst of doing a PBS series on space, and now that he had name recognition, he was being barraged with invitations to address schools, 4H groups, and graduating classes on outer space, the possibility of life beyond earth, string theory, relativity, you name it. He'd already been given half a dozen honorary degrees. I figured all he was doing was cashing in on being a good-looking black man with a degree from Harvard, a James Earl Jones voice and a knack for popularizing science. Somehow, Caleb didn't seem to see it that way.

Once Joliet had opened up the meeting for new concerns, Caleb was off and running.

"You'll all note," he stated, "that Henri is not here again."

"I think he's in Dallas," Mark said. "Doing a presentation for the school board or something."

"Or something," Caleb echoed. "It's always something. He's gallivanting around, not carrying anywhere near the teaching load the rest of us have; he's neglecting his advisor duties and his department duties. And who has to pick up the slack? Us, of course. Meanwhile, none of you guys say a thing."

He had a point, but what Caleb was really saying was, "Why not me?" I knew Caleb had grown up on the "other side of the tracks". He'd told me so on plenty of occasions: how his mother used to do other people's laundry, how they never had a house of their own. How he'd made this bargain with God when he was seven years old that if God would just let him be rich and famous, he would be a model citizen, provide for his mother and four siblings, do whatever it took. I guess God just didn't listen very well, because instead of being rich and famous, Caleb was paying alimony to two ex-wives, child support for three kids, and still living in a rented house. If he hadn't been such a prick, I'd have felt sorry for him.

Dr. Joliet broke in with, "Henri was awarded the endowed chair on his own merits. The Landauers funded it. It doesn't come out of university funds. And, furthermore, he's bringing a lot of great publicity to the department."

"Right!" Caleb went on, taking his own interpretation of the chairman's remarks. "And on top of that, he has an endowed chair! The two million the university got from the Landauers is generating interest so that he can fly around the country not worrying about writing grants he would have had to be writing like the rest of us. That two million could have been used for something useful, like a nuclear reactor."

"A nuclear reactor was never in the works," Dr. Joliet laughed.

"Give it a rest, will you?" Frank cried out. "I don't want to hear about your blood feud with Henri D'Amboise anymore."

"And then," Caleb said, glaring at Frank but not skipping a beat, "There's the quality of his research. I mean, come on! Is there life beyond earth? Let's count the planets. That's not research. That's popular science."

"Yeah, well," Walter said.

"Anyway, I say more power to him," Dana said. "He's added more to the reputation of this department than you ever have."

"Really?" Caleb said. "And what value do you add?"

"I take pride in my teaching," Dana replied, her lips trembling.

"You're a wonderful teacher, Dana," I told her. "And, anyhow, I don't think we should be discussing Henri behind his back."

"You guys are wusses," Caleb snorted. "The guy shits all over you, and all you say is thank you."

"I think we're going to have to continue this next week," Dr. Joliet said, standing up.

◊

MARK BURST INTO MY office not long after our department lunch and closed the door behind him. His normal good grooming had vanished, replaced by wild curls, red eyes, and a couple of days' worth of beard.

It's happened, I thought. I didn't relish going back through this again, but there wasn't anywhere I could possibly escape to.

"Jerry left me," Mark burst out, dropping heavily into the chair in front of my desk.

"I'm so sorry," I said from behind my desk.

"We talked, just as you suggested," Mark said in an accusatory manner. "After a nice dinner, we sat down, and I told him he didn't have to lie anymore. I knew he was cheating on me. I just wanted him to admit it."

I remember feeling responsible and oh, so guilty. Of course, neither of us could have known at the time that Jerry would be back later that year, on his knees with a bouquet of white roses and a magnum of Dom Perignon. And, unbeknownst to anyone, HIV. Oh, God, I couldn't help but think, let me change the course of this one thing.

Let me just whisper, "Don't allow him back into your life." Or maybe just "Beware" or "HIV!" Yes, let just one word change, and maybe Mark's whole life will be different.

"At first Jerry wouldn't even admit it," Mark was saying. "Instead, he turned it on its head. He said I had hurt him deeply. He accused me of having no trust in him. How, he asked me, could we have a relationship without trust?"

"That's a good one," I said.

Mark gave me a weak smile. "I guess. Well, that went on forever. When he finally stopped, I demolished his whole argument. I called it a tautological redundancy, and told him exactly where he had committed logical fallacies. I did exactly what I shouldn't have done. It didn't help my case, and all it did was get him furious.

"Jerry shot back that I had always looked down on him intellectually, that I was smug and arrogant and full of myself. I told him he was not very bright and overly emotional and a liar. So, yes, he said, he had cheated on me, not once but many, many times, but it was only because he couldn't stand being with me anymore. He couldn't even stand himself when he was with me. Not only did I look down on him intellectually, but I cramped his style with my inhibitions. I never wanted to do anything other than the old in and out, and why did he have to be the one on the bottom all the time?"

"I really don't want to hear about that part of it…," I was saying, but Mark was talking too fast to stop.

"Why couldn't we try something more exciting he said?

Other positions; bring in other partners; sunbathe naked for once in our lives on the Chelsea pier? That I was an uptight, vanilla, fuddy-duddy, old SCIENCE TEACHER. That he couldn't think of anything more boring on earth than what I did for a living.

"Well at this point, he had gotten into character assassination. In fact, I'm not a science teacher at all; I'm a physicist and an academic, but of course, Jerry doesn't make those sorts of distinctions. Then he said he couldn't imagine why he had put up with me so long, anyway, and he was so out of there. And he left."

He cradled his head in his hands.

"I'm sorry," I said again.

When Mark looked up there was fury on his face. "You should be! Who was it who counseled me to have it out with him? You!" He paused to run his fingers through his hair. "You, who are having an adulterous affair with Mimi's husband! And why should I have listened to you? You don't care about me. You're too busy having fun under tables in pizzerias!" He dropped his head back into his hands.

"That's not fair. I do care about you," I said, not denying the rest.

"Why?" Mark cried. "Jerry doesn't."

"Jerry's an idiot," I said. "You're better off without him."

From inside his fingers, a small voice emerged. "But I love him!"

Love, I thought. What grief we go through in the name of love.

Mark looked up, his eyes shiny. "I'm sorry. I've been having these crying jags. And I think I'm developing a dependence on Valium."

"Mark, don't!" I chided. "Don't let the little dweeb get to you like that!"

"Dweeb?" he said, taken by surprise. "Are you calling Jerry a dweeb?"

I remember realizing all of a sudden that I might not be able to win here. Mark could call Jerry anything he liked, but anything I said could be held against me. The problem with being a confidante is that when a friend breaks up with her lover, she'll enumerate all his worst points. Of course, you agree with her, partly because you want to convey your sympathy, and partly because you probably thought those terrible things about her ex- in the first place. But then, as it would most assuredly happen eight months later with Mark, the ex- reappears with flowers and champagne, and the one who has been left forgives, forgets and welcomes him back into his life. In the end, the confidante is left, odd man out, with the permanent stain of remembering every smear and slander, every fault and criticism.

Mark, meanwhile, was busy shouting, "Jerry's right! I'm inhibited! I'm boring! I'm a nerd! I don't want three or more people in my bed! And the thought of sunbathing nude on Chelsea Pier, surrounded by a hundred other nude men, makes me physically sick! I don't know what he ever saw in me!" At this, Mark put his head back in his hands and wept.

I had no idea what to do. Warm and fuzzy was never my style. The thought of hugging people made me shudder. But I forced myself to trade the safety of my desk for the space beside Mark's chair. Reluctantly, I put an arm around him.

"You're not boring!" I insisted. "You have a brilliant mind! And if Jerry can't appreciate that, Mark, he's not for you."

And so it went, exactly the way it had the first time. Not a word was out of place. Mark eventually calmed down and said it was probably for the best. And I said it was probably for the best, too. He said he was sorry, and he didn't hold my dalliance with Frank against me. I patted him on the shoulder, and he kissed me on the cheek. Then he left. Eight months later, Jerry came back with the flowers and the champagne and all was forgiven.

◊

IT WAS AROUND MID June. The summer semester had started, but campus was fairly quiet. Some of the professors were already enjoying their holidays. A few had a couple of classes to prepare for and to attend, but above the lush green of the quad, with clouds no more than wisps in a wide blue sky, the air fresh and sweet, none of us could keep our minds on our studies.

It was for this reason we had settled on June for our annual Physics Department barbecue and baseball game. Walter had reserved the baseball field from eleven to five and made sure that no one forgot with a weekly countdown of memos stuffed into our mail cubbyholes. He'd put up a sign-up sheet, and everyone had a responsibility: equipment, drinks, food, tableware. I brought coleslaw, the only thing I knew how to make reliably.

By the time I got there, Walter was already sweeping off the bases. Henri D'Amboise, all in white—white shirt, white pants, white shoes, except for a bright bloom of red silk tucked into his shirt pocket, was standing in the shade with a plastic tumbler in his hand. I could see Edwin, in a t-shirt that said "Save the Rainforests" and cargo shorts, busy at the food table, filling a paper plate with potato salad and something from a casserole dish. A bunch of little kids, shrieking, were chasing each other around the diamond. Two were Walter's, I knew; three were Dana's; and one fat ten-year-old boy, Ronnie, was Caleb's from his first marriage. Or maybe it was his second, I never could remember which.

A barrel full of beer sat underneath the table, complete with tap and a couple of dozen plastic cups resting on top. Watching Caleb fill his glass, Ronnie at his side, I was struck by the fact that you'd never find liquor at a university function with minors any more, the result of preventable deaths and the lawsuits that followed by furious, grieving parents.

All sorts of things would change over the next quarter century that we never would have expected, both good and bad. Just at this university alone, there would be a rape, a murder, and that epidemic of gastrointestinal flu when the whole place had to be quarantined. Of course there would also be three basketball championships, a dozen Rhodes scholars, and a Pulitzer prize-winning novelist. Stuff happened, but humans only wanted to know the good things about themselves, not the bad. Maybe that was why we really didn't want to know what the future held.

I walked over and filled a cup with beer, foam cascading up and over the top. I sucked it up before any more was lost. "Hey, Margaret," Caleb said to me, slinging one arm over my shoulder and drawing me in. "Ronnie, this is Dr. Braverman."

Ronnie shrugged. "I met you last year."

This kid rubbed me the wrong way, just like his father. "So we did," I said, stepping out from under his father's embrace. "I seem to remember you striking out," I said.

Three of the other kids came by then, scooped mounds of marshmallow fluff onto whatever they already had on their plates and ran off. Edwin came back for seconds, following Mark, who was carefully spooning a bit of this and a bit of that onto his plate, around the table. Henri filled his plate with a little of everything and stood there, plate in hand, talking to Dr. Joliet about enrollment. I grabbed a hot dog, stuck it on a bun, squeezed some French's mustard on it, and walked about, polishing it off with relish. I couldn't remember when I had last had a hot dog. Full of nitrates, salt and unmentionables; very bad for you, but so delicious! I would have had a second, but 35 seemed happy enough with one, and I couldn't snag another with the three fingers I had at my disposal. I settled for a clutch of potato chips, also naughty, salty and delicious. Never had food seemed so delectable.

A pile of metal bats lay in the dirt just outside the dugout, Walter standing just to the right with a checklist in his hand. As each of us came near, Walter sorted us onto one team or the other. I walked toward him, asking to be assigned.

"Henri—home team," he ruled. "Caleb—visitors." "Margaret—home. Ronnie—visitors. Dana—home...." As he counted us off, we were pointed into two enemy groups. We were fifteen, not counting Dr. Joliet, who said he'd sit this year out. Not counting the kids, as well. And not counting Mimi, who came decked out in a gingham dress and who parked herself fifty feet away on top of a red and white checkered tablecloth, the baby asleep in an over-the-top carriage complete with netting to keep the flies away.

I could see Frank getting up from the tablecloth, kissing Mimi and making his way toward the field.

"Mark—visitors, Elise—home; Frank—visitors...," Walter intoned, as Frank walked past. Our eyes met briefly but unobtrusively over Walter's head. Better, his eyes said, to be in opposing groups. Better they don't see us as being on the same side. Frank headed away from us, toward the food table, but I could tell from the angle of his gaze that he was still looking my way. Glancing first at Mimi, whose back was toward me as she fussed with the baby, I followed.

"Frank," I said softly, as I reached the table.

He looked up at me with a cagey grin, then quickly checked in his wife's direction. She was still turned away. "Come," he said, jerking his head toward the scoreboard, which said 0 innings 0 runs 0 hits. He put down his paper plate and headed in the direction he had indicated. For a half a minute I stood there, making a show of casually sipping my beer, before I threw it half-finished into the plastic-lined refuse pail. With one last look at Mimi's back bent over the carriage, I followed Frank behind the scoreboard.

I hardly saw him at first; he was almost completely engulfed in the long line of shadow the noon sun cast, the remnants of his grin floating, disembodied, in the dark. I aimed myself toward that smile till, at last, arms came out of nowhere to encircle me. His lips found mine in the dark, his embrace sliding lower and lower, until, clothes or no clothes, we came together.

After five minutes of this ecstatic stranglehold, Frank suddenly let go. "Oh, God," he moaned. "What am I doing?" He brushed his hand one last time against my cheek, stepped out of the shadow and was gone.

We pretended to ignore each other for the rest of the day.

Home team caucused in the dugout, where it was agreed that I would be at first base. Dana said she'd be happy to be assigned a position as far away as possible, so she got center field. Henri intoned in his usual deep authoritative tone that he would be pitching, and no one contradicted him. Over by the pitcher's mound stood the motley crew of the opposing team: a couple of instructors, Walter, a gang of kids; and Caleb arguing with Frank over something I couldn't hear.

Eventually, the teams came together at home plate to shake hands. Henri picked tails, and when Caleb's son did the coin toss, that's just what it was. Our team was at bat.

Henri put Dana up first, where she promptly struck out. Then Edwin was up and swung big, his metal bat pinging the ball way up and over Caleb's head, into left field and going, going…right into the mitt of a young instructor whose name I have managed to forget. Then Dana's oldest daughter made it to first on a grounder, leading to Henri, who, in addition to pitching, was batting clean-up. He hit the ball far into right field, and Dana's daughter came in. I was up.

I hadn't done this in twenty years, but my body felt limber and light-footed, thrilling to swing and hit and run just for the fun of it. What a day! What a day!

Caleb, with a nasty gleam in his eye, pitched, the ball coming fast and straight, but with a dip in its future trajectory I could see from a mile away. Unfortunately, 35 wasn't so prescient, so my swing was high. The next was a ball, so laughably wide that our team couldn't help but heckle the pitcher.

"Hey, Caleb," Dana shouted. "This isn't quantum mechanics! You can't pitch over there and expect it to turn up in the strike zone."

I shuffled my feet in the dust, and got back into position.

The next looked like a fastball, and it was. I pulled back and swung, the metal bat singing out, the ball whistling high into the air. I dropped the bat and ran hard, strong young legs carrying me fluidly over the dirt to first base. No clicking, no aching, no hitching up at the hip; the body doing just what it was supposed to and getting me there in plenty of time. Yes! Unfortunately, it was caught in left field and thrown to second for the third out. The other team was up.

They brought in a few runs, as did we the next inning. The lead went back and forth. By the fifth inning, our last because we only had the field till five, the teams were tied. Caleb was flagging as a pitcher. Frank wanted to relieve him, but he wouldn't give it up. Frank shrugged and went back to third. Henri hit a ball straight to Caleb's midsection, knocking the wind out of him and bouncing onto the ground. By the time he responded, Edwin was rounding second. Caleb threw to Frank, but the ball was way over his head. The guy in left field missed the ball entirely, and had to run after it. Meanwhile, Edwin rounded third and went home, our team cheering, "Victory!"

"I threw it right to you," we could hear Caleb yelling.

"You crazy? You threw it over my head," Frank yelled back.

"It was your fault we lost the game!"

"My fault? You can't throw straight!"

"Boys, boys!" Dr. Joliet said, as he came onto the field. "It's only a game."

Both of them looked over at him, glared at each other, and walked off in opposite directions.

They could have been fighting about anything: baseball, physics, grants, or who was the more popular teacher. It didn't matter what. Caleb was out to get Frank, and Frank hated Caleb's guts. At the time, I remember, I thought they were fighting over me. From the mature point of view of my sixty years, twenty-five long years after today happened, however, I would say that that, if true, it was not a good thing. But on that very day—either the first time I lived it or the second, with the sun warm on my back, high on endorphins and beer and love, it was glorious.

CHAPTER 11

THERE WAS A KNOCK at the front door of my lab. I wondered who this could be. Any of the students would know to just come in; that was true, too, of Frank or Caleb. If I were there, I'd probably have my hands full with whatever I was doing and certainly wouldn't want to drop everything to open the door. Besides, the door was never locked.

"Come in!" I called.

The door cracked open, revealing the big hair and hoop earrings of Janie Carr. "Am I interrupting something, Dr. Braverman?" she asked.

I was right in the middle of setting up a new experiment. I had the entire design in my head and all I wanted to do was to be allowed enough uninterrupted time to lay what was in my head out on the table. I lifted my eyes from the set-up long enough to look up at her. "What do you think?" I asked.

Janie must have thought that meant no, because she opened the door wide and waltzed in, dressed in some psychedelic concoction of yellow tank top and purple jeans that all but blew my eyes out. "I thought you might have some time to show me around your lab," she said.

"Do you see I'm in the midst of something?" I said, returning my attention to the apparatus.

"Oh, it won't take a minute," Janie said, pulling out her notebook and pointing it at the apparatus. "What's that thingamabob you've got there?"

I sighed. "It's a Mach-Zehnder interferometer. It takes an incoming light pulse from a laser, splits it in two with a half-silvered mirror, and sends the two halves over different paths and recombines them."

"Really?" she said, writing. "How do you spell Mach-Zehnder?"

"M-A-C-H. Forget it. If you're really interested I can send you a flyer from the manufacturer," I said, not looking up.

"That'll work. Send it to the *Garriston News* office." She leaned over my shoulder. So what's the experiment about?"

"Look, this is really not a good time, Miss Carr."

"No prob. I can wait," Janie said, pulling over a lab stool and sitting down.

I went back to calibrating the instrument. I could hear her fidgeting, standing up, walking around, flopping down again.

After a few more minutes of this, my concentration was shot. "What is it I can help you with, Ms. Carr?" I asked, turning my head in her direction.

"Well, I just wanted to get to know what you're doing here," she said, grabbing her notebook and flipping to a blank page.

"I'm planning to test Wheeler's delayed-choice experiment in quantum mechanics."

"Quantum what?"

I sighed and stood up. "Maybe you'd better come back after taking Physics 101. "

To her credit, Janie laughed. "Okay, maybe I better just ask you some questions."

"Fine," I said, leaning back against the table, my arms crossed against my chest. I'd give her a short interview, 35 was surely thinking, and then she'll go away.

"IF you had a working time machine," Janie began, "would it be anything like the one in *The Time Machine* by H.G. Wells?"

I couldn't help but laugh. "That was a purely fictional device. Wells hardly described the apparatus in the book, as I remember."

"The book?" Janie said, a bewildered look in her eyes. "Oh. I never read the book. I mean the movie. It was this big shiny vehicle—with a leather seat and a clock mechanism and, I think, a gyroscope."

I shook my head. This is why I never talked to the press. If you could call Janie Carr the press.

"But there IS a vehicle?" Janie insisted.

I didn't comment. What was the point? She'd twist whatever I said.

"So there ISN'T a vehicle?"

I just looked at her.

"Well, then," Janie said, jumping off the stool, "how about *Somewhere in Time*, where this guy THINKS himself back to this luxury hotel in San Diego in 1896."

"Another movie…?" I asked. A prickle of irritation passed through me.

"Yeah, a wonderful one with Christopher Reeve and Jane Seymour."

For several minutes she gushed over how romantic the story had been, and how Christopher Reeve was such a hunk, what a gorgeous couple the two made. I wondered briefly whether Christopher Reeve was still unhurt in 1987 and decided he was. What a shock that had been. What a tragedy.

"Christopher Reeve may be gorgeous, but you've got to admit that thinking yourself back in time is pretty ridiculous," 35 was saying.

"Well, okay. Then there's a book called *Time and Again,*" Janie said, pacing back and forth, reading from her notebook, "by Jack Finney, where he was drafted into this secret US government project to HYPNOTIZE himself into going back to 1880s New York City." She stopped pacing. "Is your project financed by the military?"

"No, it's not financed by the military," I said, laughing.

The corners of Janie's lips turned upwards. "You've just acknowledged there **is** a project."

Adrenalin coursed through my system, but 35 got it under control. "I didn't do any such thing, Ms. Carr," I said. "And I'm losing patience here. You have no evidence of any project. You're just on some silly fishing expedition."

"I'll bypass that for the moment," Janie said, waving the issue away with her hand. "But my question is this." Long pause, with full frontal eye contact. "Can you hypnotize yourself back into time?"

I must have hesitated. Hypnosis isn't a form of unconsciousness as many people think. It's an altered state where the subject is fully awake and hyper-focusing her attention. How different did that actually sound from what I had done? In fact, even I—60—who had successfully transported myself through time, could be forgiven if I still entertained the smallest doubt that I was hallucinating the whole thing. Imagine the reaction of 35, who had yet to see the theory in action.

"No," I said after a millisecond or two. "That's ridiculous."

"Aha!" Janie said, jumping up. "Then it's true! That's just what you're doing!"

I stiffened. 35 had been caught by surprise. She shouldn't have been. That had always been where Janie was going with this. Janie didn't understand the underlying science. She didn't care to. All she wanted was to trap me into giving her some silly, sensational story, and damn the details.

"No," I said firmly. "It is not true. You cannot send yourself back in time through self-hypnosis. There is no time travel project. What I am working on is a project on Wheeler's delayed-choice, and it is getting late. So, if you don't mind, Ms. Carr, I'm going to get back to work."

I got up and opened the front door, but Janie didn't take the hint. Instead, she began to walk in the opposite direction, toward the backroom door. She even tried the knob, but it was locked. "This is where you do the time travel, isn't it?" she said. "Show me what's inside."

"This is a supply closet," I said, going over to her and grabbing her arm. "And the only time involved is that yours is up." I led her forcibly to the front door and closed the door behind her.

◊

THE FOLLOWING DAY, JUST as I was getting back into setting up the lab apparatus, the door swung open. It was Caleb. I said he never knocked. His expression was strange: smug, like the cat that swallowed the canary. Well, maybe that wasn't so strange for Caleb, after all.

"You have a minute, Margaret?" he asked.

My hands were busy in the equipment, and again, all I wanted to do was to be allowed enough uninterrupted time to lay what was in my head out on the table. I lifted my eyes from the set-up long enough to look up at him. "Does it look like I have a minute?" I asked.

Caleb chuckled but didn't comment. He just pulled over the same lab stool that Janie had commandeered the day before and sat down. "You'll want to know, I think, that Janie Carr came over to talk to me yesterday afternoon."

"Will I?" I said, not looking up, though my body was already reacting to his words with a shiver of fear. Both Janie Carr and Caleb Winter were loose cannons. That the two of them were colluding at something wasn't a happy prospect.

"Isn't that a Mach-Zehnder interferometer?" Caleb asked, looking over my shoulder.

"Yes," I answered, finally straightening up.

"What are you using it for?"

I took a deep breath and prayed for patience. "I found a way to test Wheeler's Delayed-Choice paradigm."

"Very interesting. The interferometer should let the photon take either...."

Enough was enough. "Caleb, what did Janie tell you?"

Caleb spun the stool around like a boy at a soda fountain. "Nice. I think I'll have to buy me one of these."

I put my hands on my hips and looked him in the eye. "Please, Caleb. I'd like to get back to work before dinnertime." The position and the sarcasm worked well with my students. I had hoped it might here, too.

Caleb only shrugged. "So, Janie came in with this theory," he said, smiling. "Seems she's convinced you're still working on time travel."

I shrugged my shoulders as casually as I could. "I wouldn't put too much credence in what Janie Carr thinks."

"I grant you that Janie's not exactly an expert," Caleb said, as he spun the stool around again, "but her wacky ideas reminded me a little of what you said at the department meeting. You know, sending your conscious self back in time. What Janie said was that you were hypnotizing yourself back in time."

"You don't believe her, do you?" I asked, my heart thumping to a salsa beat.

"Actually, I do kind of believe her," Caleb said. "Not her theory so much as her conviction that you haven't stopped the experiment. You told her the backroom is a supply closet, when we both know that's where you practically blew yourself up a couple of months ago."

"Well, now it's a supply closet."

"Then you'd be willing to show me what's in there?"

"Listen, Caleb. I'm really busy…," I tried, but it bounced right off him.

"In fact, Janie's convinced that you succeeded. Now, I'd love to see the evidence of that. Think what it would mean to the department. To the world," Caleb said, a not-so-friendly smirk on his lips.

I remembered this moment well. I knew that he'd already seen a picture of my apparatus in the campus newspaper, after Frank and I had neglected to lock the door to the backroom, and the cleaning lady got scared and called Security. There was no other evidence. The machine hadn't worked the first time, as far as 35 knew, and it didn't work the last time. It was a failure in everyone's mind except my own. I remember thinking, what was there to see? Best to just open the door and let him see for himself.

I took out my key chain and found the key among a medley of others: class room, building, house, car. I walked over and unlocked the backroom door.

"Be my guest," I said, walking in, my arms outstretched to signify the entire room.

Caleb followed. He inspected the chair, the hood, the

electrode-like wiring. He examined the timing mechanism, the black button, the electrical connections.

"Well?" I asked after what seemed like forever. I knew 35 was expecting a reproach on how this whole contraption was science fiction at best; how could I possibly expect consciousness to defy time? But that wasn't what was about to happen at all. Oh God, I remembered this part all oh so well, but I still couldn't do anything to change it.

All of a sudden, Caleb reached behind me and pushed the door closed. Then he turned to me and, as if planned, grabbed me by the waist, drawing me to him, one hand creeping down into the waist band of my pants.

I tried to shove him away, but his hold on me was too strong. I grabbed his hair and pulled, but all this accomplished was to temporarily reroute the hand in my pants to break the grip of my hand on his hair. I tried to scream, but his lips were sealed to mine in a fierce kiss. All I could do was knee him in the testicles, but it was a glancing blow, and he grabbed hold of me again, shoved me into the chair, where he held me fast with one hand. At the time I remember being surprised at his strength.

"Margaret," Caleb panted. "All I want is a little of what Frank gets."

"Then go call Mimi," I said, struggling. "Frank and I are just friends."

"I don't believe that for one second."

"Believe what you want. If you think I'd ever have sex with you, Frank or no Frank, you're delusional."

"I've wanted you from the first day I saw you," he said, his eyes lit with lust.

"You have a funny way of showing it," I replied, my hand on his chest and shoving as hard as I could. But it had no effect. His lips were now deep inside my blouse, his tongue exploring my cleavage.

My lips, however were free. I began to scream at the top of my lungs, "Rape! Rape! Help! Help!" The words echoed around the little room: "Rape,rape,rape,rape,rape… help,help,help,help,help." It was pretty clear they weren't going anywhere—that damned soundproofing, again. In fact, all it managed to accomplish was to get Caleb to lift his head up and laugh.

"Nobody will hear you," he said. "Not in this building."

When I began again Caleb didn't even try to stop me. "Help me, help me, help me, help me, help me," reverberated around the room for a minute until it died out. It was futile.

"Be nice, Margaret," he chided. "Or I'll be forced to tell Joliet you're continuing the experiment, against his express orders."

I almost laughed. "You don't think I'll tell him about this? You suppose he'll think my experiment is more criminal than your attacking me?"

"It's your word against mine," Caleb said as he pulled down my pants. "I'll tell him you offered your body in return for my not telling him what I know."

"Joliet's smarter than that."

"Joliet will take my word against yours any day. Anyway, Joliet's not going to be chair forever. Play nice with me, Margaret, and I'm sure we can work something out...."

I had known about this incident for twenty-five years, and longed to get even with him for it, but now that I was here, all I could do was what I had done before. I bit his lip hard enough to draw blood then kneed him in the balls when he slackened his grip on me. I considered locking him in as I ran out, but was afraid that the longer he sat in that little room, the more likely it was that he would sabotage my machine. So in the end, history repeated itself. As Caleb crouched there, doubled over in pain, I ran out of the room, 35 hoping against hope that Joliet would take my side over his.

◊

I WAS ALREADY IN DR. Joliet's office by the time Caleb staggered in, breathless and disheveled. His lip was split and he was still hobbling a little from the pain in his groin. Granted, I wasn't exactly looking my best either. My blouse had bloodstains on it from when I'd bitten him, and, though I'd tucked it back into my pants, I must have looked a sight. By then I'd given Joliet my side of the story. Caleb had, for no reason I could see, attacked me in my lab. I'd fought back and run straight here.

"Did she tell you that she's still working on that goddamned experiment?" Caleb asked when he regained his breath.

Joliet, who was already looking a little gray around the gills—whether from the cancer that was eating him up from the inside out, or from the prospect of a tawdry sex scandal I wouldn't know—acknowledged that I had not said anything about that.

"First of all," I interjected, "Caleb is making that up. He has no evidence whatsoever about that. He's just...."

"Don't believe her. She's lying," Caleb said with great self-righteousness. "She offered her body to me in return for my not telling you what I know."

For a second I stood there stunned. The guy would say anything. "What?" I managed to get out before Joliet began speaking.

"Is this true?" he asked me.

"You're not going to chastise him about attacking me?!" I cried.

"First things first," Joliet said, grabbing a tissue from a small square box on the corner of his desk to mop his brow. "Are you still engaging in the time travel experiment?"

"No," I said, deciding that lying under the circumstances was the only thing to do.

"You're sure?" he asked.

"I can't believe this. No," I said. "I am not engaging in the time travel experiment."

"Then you didn't offer your body to Caleb in return for...," Joliet said, mopping his brow again, "Caleb's... um...silence?"

"I can't believe you're questioning me about this, and

Caleb is getting off scot-free. Why don't you ask him if he attacked me?"

"No one said he's getting off scot-free. Please answer my question, Margaret."

Through the corner of my eye I could see Caleb standing there, a grin on his swollen lips. "Look at him," I shrieked. "He's smirking, for God's sake. No, I definitely did NOT offer my body to that piece of shit over there."

"Language, young woman," Joliet scolded. He turned toward Caleb, who was still grinning. "Now, Caleb, how did you get that swollen lip?"

"I bit him," I interrupted. "Of course! He was attacking me!"

"Hold on, hold on, Margaret. I'm asking Caleb."

"Margaret bit me," Caleb answered.

"On what provocation?" Joliet asked.

"On what provocation?" I shouted. "I just told you."

Joliet turned to me, mopping his brow one last time with the tissue, before throwing it in the trash bin under his desk. "Margaret, be quiet!"

It felt like we were in grade school, and all Caleb had done was to pull my pigtail.

"I came into her lab unexpectedly," Caleb said calmly, "and found Margaret in her backroom, firing up, so to speak, her so-called time machine. I asked her what she was doing, and she kind of sidled up to me and offered herself, saying that if I didn't say anything about this, she'd be happy to take care of me in any way she could."

As stunned as I was by this total bullshit, I managed to say, "No! That wasn't what happened at all!"

Joliet leaned over and grabbed another tissue from the box. "Caleb, do you swear that your version is correct?"

"I do," Caleb said.

"Do you, Margaret?"

I must have hesitated, recalling that I had had to lie when I said that I wasn't continuing the experiment, so my answer of, "Absolutely!" came a split second late. Both of them looked at me with pity.

I think it was Hitler who said, "The bigger the lie, the more people will believe it." What I have learned in my 60 years on the planet is that the people who lie the biggest—the psychopaths and the madmen, the ones who delude themselves into believing their own lie or who have no capacity for guilt—those are the people who get away with murder. It's us little sinners, the ones who lie seldom and lie small, who quibble or misspeak, who feel guilt and then stew about it, unable to clear their conscience, who get caught.

"I'd say this is a classic case of he said/she said," Joliet was saying. "I seriously urge the two of you to reach some sort of amicable agreement here, because if I'm forced to turn it over to the Grievance Committee, it will without a doubt be thrown out for lack of evidence. And meanwhile, there will be a major hullaballoo, and it won't bode well for either of you—you for your promotion, Caleb, and you, Margaret, for your job. Not to mention the department as a whole."

Both Caleb and I looked on in silence. God, I remember this, I—60—was thinking. I'd somehow thought that Joliet had yet to come to the point. My silence didn't mean that I had no objections. Say something! Now! I screamed from inside my head. But 35 was still waiting for Joliet to go on.

"Good," Dr. Joliet said, throwing the second tissue into the trash bin. "I expect to hear no more about it."

◊

ON TUESDAY AFTERNOON, THE usual stack of *Garriston News* appeared in the lobby of the science building. I was almost afraid to look at it, but I picked one up on my way upstairs. There, on the second page was the story I feared:

PHYSICS PROF CLAIMS TIME TRAVEL PROJECT NOT FINANCED BY MILITARY

As of August 6, all that is left in physics Professor Braverman's front lab is a cryptic set-up of prisms and cables, along with a curious piece of equipment called an interferometer which splits light in two. As for the back-room, which early last May revealed evidence of a fire and of a strange machine, the professor barred all entry to it.

Dr. Braverman insisted that her project was not financed by the military, but, asked whether she

had used self-hypnosis to transport herself back into time, she
hesitated for many moments before
making a strong show of denying
it. So many mysteries remain, and
Dr. Braverman seems unwilling to
shed light on any of them!

CHAPTER 12

WHEN I WAS SEVENTEEN, I told my parents I wanted to be a scientist. My father, the businessman, said I should go into the arts. That's what he had always wanted to do but had to give it up to make a living.

My mother, the teacher, said I should be a teacher. If you had a teacher's diploma, she told me, you'll always have something to fall back on.

Why did I need a back-up plan? I asked her. Did she think I was going to fail?

Your mother has your best interests at heart, my father said. Why don't you just listen for a change?

My guidance counselor advised me gently that girls don't do math, even when said girl had just received a 754 on her Math SAT. Instead, Mrs. Kolchok suggested, with my mathematical bent I could surely be a bank teller or a science teacher or maybe even, since Medicine intrigued me, a nurse.

I pondered all this unsolicited advice for about a year. I weighed my parents' experience against my own passion. I set Mrs. Kolchok's advice against my own inner voice. I weighed and I sifted and I measured. And when the year was done, I knew the answer: I must not listen to anyone but myself.

My father would probably tell you, by the way, that I

never listened to anyone else anyway.

So it was with this in mind that I decided to ignore Dr. Joliet's clear admonition that he didn't want to hear any more about the Caleb affair. Instead, I petitioned the University Grievance Committee to hear the case. And three and a half weeks later, to Dr. Joliet's chagrin, Caleb and I were called to appear at the Grievance hearing.

We were ushered into the old conference room in the administration building, the way it used to be before they renovated it with every tech option imaginable; before it became wireless everything, with large pull-down screens for high-definition video conferencing and pop-up data ports, one for every ergonomic leather chair that lined the sides of the table.

Back again were the pristine white walls, punctuated here and there by a tasteful print and a dozen high-backed chairs encircling a long seamless shiny table with no place to plug anything in. Seated on the far side of this long table was a panel of five people: three men and two women, each with pristine yellow legal pads in front of them. The administrative officer, Dr. Gonzalez, a dark middle-aged man with a paunch, sat in the middle.

I, the grievant, was invited to sit down across from them to their left and Caleb to their right. The whole thing was very solemn and professional. Dr. Gonzalez introduced us to himself and the other four members, two appointed by the president and three elected by the faculty council. He unscrewed the cap on his Waterman's fountain pen and aligned it carefully with the edge of his yellow legal pad. Then he began the proceedings.

"Today we are hearing the grievance by Dr. Margaret Braverman against Dr. Caleb Winter, both of the Physics Department. Dr. Braverman contends that Dr. Winter attacked her in the backroom of her lab. We'll begin with Dr. Braverman making her case. Dr. Braverman?"

"Well, Your Honor, uh, Dr. Gonzalez. I was in my lab setting up an experiment…"

"On what date would that be?" asked one of the committee members.

"It was the afternoon of August 7."

"Thank you. Go on," Dr. Gonzalez said, writing something on his pad.

"Well, Caleb, uh, Dr. Winter just barged in…"

"The door was unlocked," Caleb said. "It's natural for colleagues to go in and out…"

"Dr. Winter, please," Dr. Gonzalez said. "You will have your turn. Dr. Braverman, please continue."

"Well, he started accusing me of continuing an experiment that I, uh, was not doing. Caleb—uh, Dr. Winter asked me to let him into my backroom so he could see for himself, and, well, I had nothing to hide, so I did. He looked around for a few minutes and suddenly, out of the blue, he shoved the door closed and attacked me."

"How exactly did he attack you?" one of the members asked.

"I didn't attack her," Caleb said.

Dr. Gonzalez looked at him sharply, and Caleb shut up.

"Well," I said. "He shoved his hand down my pants, and his tongue into my cleavage." At this the two female committee members gasped.

"I asked him to stop," I went on, "but he wouldn't. I couldn't break his hold, so, uh, I bit him in the lip and kneed him in the groin." Here, the two male committee members winced.

"I got away and ran out straight to Dr. Joliet, our department chairman."

"Is that it?" Dr. Gonzalez asked, his pen poised in the air.

"Isn't that enough?" I said.

"Are there any witnesses to Dr. Winter's alleged attack?" one of the committee members asked.

"No," I said. "Do you think he would have done it if there were anyone around?"

"Dr. Braverman, I think we can conduct this a little more civilly."

"Sorry, but it was a miserable experience."

There was silence for half a minute until Dr. Gonzalez asked, "Any other questions for the grievant?"

The committee members shook their heads.

"Then we can now proceed to the respondent's case. Dr. Winter?"

"What actually happened," Caleb said, giving the panel an unctuous smile, "was that I came into her lab unexpectedly and found Dr. Braverman in her backroom, working on her so-called time machine. I asked her what she was doing, and she offered herself, saying that if I didn't say anything about this, she'd be happy to take care of me in any way she could."

"Oh," said one of the women.

"It's not true," I snapped. "Actually, in the middle of attacking me, he said, "Be nice, Margaret, or I'll be forced to tell Joliet you're continuing the experiment, against his express orders."

"Please Dr. Braverman. You've already had your chance. Do you have any more to say, Dr. Winter?"

"Only that I would never do such a thing as I'm accused of. This is a terrible, libelous accusation, made with no evidence, and, honestly, I feel as if *I* am the victim here."

"You, the victim?" I cried, ready to throttle him.

"Please, Dr. Braverman," Dr. Gonzalez scolded. "You are not helping your case. Now, are there any other questions?"

"I'd like to ask a question of the grievant, please," said one of the members. "This time machine that Dr. Winter mentioned—does it work?"

What could I answer to that? Yes, it works, but that would certainly wrench the topic from the attack. Fortunately, 35 answered it for me. "No," she said. "It is not working yet."

Another two or three questions were raised about the time machine, until Dr. Gonzalez raised his hand. "This is not the matter under consideration. My concern is rather whether the grievant has presented sufficient credible evidence to sustain the grievance. Dr. Braverman, given that Dr. Winter disputes your claim, I have to ask you, do you have any other evidence for us?"

I thought hard, and, other than a few marks within my cleavage that I would rather not show, I could think of nothing. It had surely happened. In fact, it had happened twice. But there was no physical proof. "No, Your Honor," I said.

"Excuse us for a minute," Dr. Gonzalez said, standing up. The others stood up as well and followed him out of the conference room. That left Caleb and me alone.

"You the victim?" I said again, glowering across the table.

"No one will believe you," he said.

"We'll see about that," I shot back. Poor 35. She really thought she had a chance.

"No one," he said, turning away.

We waited another few minutes, facing in opposite directions, until the door opened and the panel reassembled themselves in their respective chairs.

"Dr. Braverman," Dr. Gonzalez declared, slowly screwing the cap back onto his Waterman's fountain pen, "as much as it pains me to say so, the lack of both evidence and witnesses forces me to dismiss this grievance."

I sat there a few moments in utter disbelief, before pushing my chair back and standing up. At that moment, my faith in due process gone forever, all I wanted was to get out of there as fast as possible. I turned on my heels and blindly rushed out the door, across the lobby and through the front entrance, searching for fresh air.

Instead, I found myself in the midst of a bunch of demonstrators. Faculty, students, and from the unfamiliar look of them, professional protesters, were marching round and round the entrance. Some brandished signs saying, "Get out of South Africa!" and "Stop apartheid!" Some yelled up at the President's windows for the university to divest itself of all its South African investments or be part of the problem. "President Cooley, what's the word?" they chanted. "Garriston's not Johannesburg."

At the head of the parade was Edwin, of course, who grinned at me as I rushed by. I smiled back, but that was just because I liked Edwin, not that I cared one way or the other, and moved on quickly. Being against apartheid was a no-brainer, but I wasn't much in the mood to support someone else's cause. Maybe I'd have been more interested if they were protesting the glass ceiling or abused women or the impossibility of getting justice from grievance committees.

My car was parked in back of MacArthur Hall, so I headed across campus. 35 seemed to be in a fog, noticing nothing, almost colliding with a beefy guy in Birkenstocks and cut-offs holding a crudely lettered sign.

"Hey," he shouted after me, but I just raced on. I could tell from the churning feeling in my stomach and my frenetic pace from one end of campus to the other how upset 35 was. It would take a long time to come to grips with my powerlessness in the face of the old status quo at the university. Years, it would take, if ever. Okay, maybe I never did come to grips with it. I just stopped thinking about it.

But in those days I still cared. I had truly believed, after the sixties, that we had changed the world. Men and women together. No more glass ceiling. No more macho power trips. The times, they are a changing. But we weren't there yet. Not in 1987. Not in 2012.

Schopenhauer Hall, the old business building, was in the process of being razed. They'd moved the business faculty out and dispersed them across campus for the time it would take to pull it all down and build it back up. 1987 was a good year for fundraising as I remember. Garriston had raised a ton of money from yuppie alums who were busy doing leveraged buyouts and hostile takeovers, not counting the cool million it got just for sticking a new name on the front. The old brick building, maybe fifty years old at the time, was standing there sad and empty as I whizzed by, square and solid and functional, but not, I guess, up to the standards of the high-flying eighties business community. In a couple of weeks some demolition company would strategically stick some dynamite into its basement and poof! the whole thing would drop to rubble in a plume of dust. Only to rise again as a steel and glass nonentity, now known as the Ingrassia Business Building, mammoth and looming and in-your-face but somehow lacking the humble integrity of its old square self. There's progress for you.

I sprinted past the Psychology Building, that long line of sixties extruded cement, which looked almost exactly the same no matter what decade you observed it from, though maybe it looked a little less like a big mistake when you saw it only two decades after it had been built. Or maybe not.

A facilities worker in headphones atop a tractor was busy mowing the green in big lazy circles, the roar of the motor cutting through the summer hush.

A twenty-something student went by in rainbow suspenders and a Sony Walkman in his pocket, the wire from it rising to a button in his ear. "Hello, Dr. Braverman," he said, raising his hand in greeting. 35 smiled back. I assumed I must have known this kid at some time in the past, but I certainly had no clue now.

I ran past the science building, past old Fine Arts Hall with its beautiful Art Noveau façade, before they tore it down and made it into another victim of progress. I ran back, back in time to the old forum of original buildings, back toward the comfort of MacArthur Hall, with its red brick cupola, clock tower, spires, a place that never had and never would change, a humble old place that always made me feel all was right with the world.

What I was running from or to, I don't know. All I know is that I wanted respect. I wanted to be appreciated and believed in. I wanted to love and be loved. But at 35, I felt as if none of that would ever come.

I ran blindly until I suddenly found myself standing

in front of a door labeled *Frank Mermonstein, Professor of Physics*. I had had no intention of coming here; perhaps I was simply drawn by the sweet scent of love. Through the rippled glass I could just make out a figure at a desk. I tried the door and it opened. "Frank," I said.

He looked up in surprise. "Margaret."

We stood there gazing at each other for a minute or so till he waved me over to a single shabby chair. I was too antsy to sit, however. I leaned over the desk, instead.

"Where the hell do we stand, Frank?" I said, glowering at him.

Frank gave me one long look before crossing the room. He glanced right, then left into the hallway and closed the door. He gestured once again for me to seat myself in the ragged old chair, and I sat. Finally, he lowered himself down behind the desk, putting as much distance between the two of us as possible. Only then did he speak.

"Who do you think you are, stalking in here like that?" Frank scolded.

I jumped up again and planted my palms on the desk in front of me. "Who do I think I am?" I shouted. "It doesn't seem to matter to anyone what I think! It's what *they* think! And *they* seem to think I'm the doo-doo under the world's collective foot! *They* can do anything they damn well like with me, but God forbid I stand up for myself, then it's `be a good little girl and don't rock the boat!' Who do I think I am?! Nobody, that's who!" I cried, dropping back into the chair.

"Who is this *they* you're talking about?" Frank asked, puzzled.

I'm sorry," I mumbled. "I'm upset. I shouldn't have come here at all." I made a motion to stand up.

"No, now that you're here, let's talk this out. Why are you so upset?"

I shrugged. As crazy as I felt, I knew I was bound by the grievance committee decision not to tell anyone what took place inside. "It doesn't matter why," I said. "Something happened that brought out all my own insecurities. I didn't even intend to come here. It just happened. Sorry."

Frank came around the desk and sat on the corner, taking my hand in his. "If this is about me, Margaret, I've already told you where I stand. Nothing has changed."

If I could have, I would have calmed down, but my body was running hot. I remember thinking that I hadn't run all the way here to be told that nothing had changed. "How," I demanded, "can you embrace me behind a scoreboard and then revert to being a complete stranger? How can you kiss me under the table, then run right back to Mimi? Why do you blow so hot and then so cold? Why?" I gave him a look of pure misery. "I never know where you stand, Frank."

"You're right, you're right," Frank said, unexpectedly. "My words tell you one thing, and my actions another." He looked up into my eyes. "It's guilt, Margaret. Compulsion and guilt. You know how I feel about you, how crazy in love with you I am. I tell myself to leave you alone. But then you appear, and I just can't help myself. We give in to our passion. It's wonderful!" He sighed. "Except then I feel guilty, and the whole process starts again."

"You know I love you, too, Frank," I said. By now I had stood up, and he had stood up, and the two of us were touching.

He took my head in his hands and kissed me softly on the mouth, then with more force. I put my arms around his middle and gently pulled him to me. He did the same, moaning a little as we came together.

"No," he said at last, taking a resolute step backwards.

I groaned and dropped back into the chair. "Why are you fighting this?"

"Don't, Margaret. Don't make this harder for me."

"Is it so important that you'll sacrifice…?" I took a look at his face, which was contorted in pain. "Fine," I said. "Just do one more thing for me, and I'll never ask anything from you again."

"Anything," he said.

"I fixed the machine. I'm sure I did. There were a few logical inconsistencies in the wiring. That had to be the problem. I need you to help me one last time, Frank. One last time."

He was quiet for a long time, thinking thoughts that I had no way of accessing. At last he said, "Okay. The least I can do for you is that. Tell me when."

CHAPTER 13

TRY, TRY AGAIN.

We first set out to test our helmet prototype in the fall of eighty-six. Ever since our first session in the dirty donut, I'd been setting aside every possible dollar of my salary to fund the project. With Frank's help I spent two years working up the specs for the machine, designing the components and shopping them out to three separate and far-flung sources. The helmet shell was built in a factory in Atlanta, the sensors in Cincinnati, and the lead shield in Lansing, Michigan. No one, if I could help it, would ever be able to follow our paper trail but Frank and me.

By nine that September night, the building was dead quiet; most everyone who had a life had gone home to it. I was busy working in the backroom of my lab, sitting in what was to become the time-travel chair, plugging sensors into the helmet when Frank let himself in with the duplicate key I'd had made for him.

I could hear the squeak of his shoes as he crossed the tile floor; the metallic clank of a hanger in the closet; the squeak of his shoes again. Then Frank appeared in the threshold, toting a cage of gray and white rabbit fur: our test subject.

"How's it coming?" Frank asked me, setting the load down on the floor. A little black nose poked its way through the crosshatching to sniff the air.

"Almost finished," I answered, upending the quarter-size mock-up helmet to reveal seventy-eight magnetic sensors, each the size and approximate shape of sugar cubes, lining the interior like bubble-wrap.

Each sensor was devised to measure infinitesimal magnetic fields in the brain by means of a coil of superconducting wire. The field would be funneled through to a quantum mechanical device that produced a voltage proportional to the field, and then the voltage patterns could be converted into maps of brain activity. The design was so straightforward it just had to work.

I finished cramming in the last few devices. The shell had been delivered last month, the lead cooling shield last week, and the superconducting devices just this morning. We aimed to put them together and to test the helmet tonight. Proof of concept was what we were looking for: that a unique mental signature could be projected onto its future counterpart. A rabbit would do as a stand-in for me.

Frank had already quietly rewired the room so we would have the abundant power we needed. I'd had no grant money for this and figured we'd just have to get along with what we had, siphoning off current from the other labs that wouldn't be using it at night. We were pretty sure that we'd have enough, though, barring any mishaps, catastrophes or snafus.

"Ready," I said, in a fever of excitement.

I belted our squirming little astrobunny securely into

the chair and snapped the miniature helmet onto his head, furry ears threaded through two small slits in the top. We plugged the machine in. Then we turned it on.

An aura of light appeared briefly around the bunny's head, then CRACK! The lights went out. Everywhere.

"It must have shorted the whole system out," Frank said from the dark.

"Damn. I guess we needed more power, after all."

"You have a flashlight?"

Just then the emergency power went on. A thin sliver of light under the door led me to the doorknob, and I turned it. Though our back cubicle was pitch-black, a triangle of light from the main lab's ceiling fixture illuminated the rabbit, shivering and twitching and blinking in fear. I remember thinking that Mr. Cottontail may not have gone anywhere, but at least I wasn't going to have to bury him that night in my backyard.

"I'm going down to the mechanical room to reset the circuit breaker," Frank told me.

"Okay," I said, hoisting the helmet above the rabbit's ears. His little red eyes, reappearing from under the hood, accused me of any number of infernal, villainous crimes against his kind. He wasn't dead, but he sure didn't look happy. And sure enough, the moment I unbelted him, he hopped down from the table and took off into the main lab. I decided he couldn't go far. I sat down and waited for Frank to get back.

Yes, it was a setback, I remember thinking, but it was

temporary. We'd buy the supplementary power supply we should have bought in the first place, and then we'd try again. In those days, I was unbowed and undaunted. If I could manage to convince myself that in theory something should work, I'd prove it or die trying.

I have to say that over time, my philosophy has become less dogmatic. Whether that's good or bad, I'm not sure. But today I'd probably say that *in theory*, anything can work. Unfortunately, *in practice*, anything can happen.

A few minutes later Frank opened the door. "The mechanical room is locked," he said. He peered into the backroom. "Where'd the rabbit go?"

Into the future, I would have liked to have told him, but I didn't. "Escaped," I said, instead.

Frank pointed to two red eyes twitching under a bench in the corner. "Here little rabbit," he crooned, crouching down to scoop it up. At the last minute, it slipped from his grasp. I ran after it from one direction, Frank from the other, hoping to trap it in a pincer movement, but it found a middle way and sequestered itself in another corner. At last Frank charged at it, forcing it into my arms, and I stuffed it unceremoniously into its cage. I would try again with that same rabbit a month later with better results.

By now it was near midnight, and we were both exhausted. I collapsed onto the lab stool. Frank leaned up against the wall. The ceiling fixture wasn't putting out a lot of light, but there was a full moon beaming in through the window. A swathe of dust motes sparkled from the window to the floor.

"We'll try it again next week after I get a separate power supply," I said.

"Well," Frank said, pausing. "You may have to go on without me."

I twirled around on the stool. "Why?" I asked. "You've got something better to do?"

Maybe it was the half-light that made his face look so sad.

"Margaret," he began.

I twirled around again. "Yes?"

"I've got to tell you something."

This wasn't really like Frank at all. If he had something to say, usually he came right out with it instead of giving me this excruciatingly slow-mo prelude.

"Spit it out, Frank," I said.

"I want you to know that I really, really like you...."

I remember that moment—it was so unexpected. For a split second a feeling of absurd joy bubbled up in me. Could this be a proposal, I remember wondering, conveniently forgetting that he already had a girlfriend. Forgetting the experiment. Forgetting time travel. Forgetting my goddamned career. All I saw in my mind was the two of us driving away in a big black car with cans on the back. What a fool I was!

"But I'm getting married," he said, wrenching his jacket from the closet and shoving one arm into it, then the other.

"You and...?" Me? I was thinking. What a fool, what a fool.

"Mimi."

Me? Me? I asked myself. Mimi? It didn't make any sense.

"When?" I wanted to know.

"October 5."

"That soon?" I wailed, my heart contracting into a tight, painful knot.

Frank came over and looked down at me—poignantly, tenderly, something about his expression not quite in tune with the occasion. If he were getting married, one might have expected elation, but this looked more like grief.

"Of course, I'll be here for the final test. That won't change," Frank said slowly.

"So soon?" I moaned, still stuck on the date. I remember thinking this was the end of the world! How could Frank marry someone else? And so soon! I lifted my hand to his cheek, but he backed away, leaving my hand dangling in the air.

"It's not so soon," he explained. "We've been going out for two years."

"Why now, then?" I asked. I was being unreasonable, of course. Getting married after two years together was not so soon. But why not four years? I asked myself. Or eight?

"Mimi's pregnant," Frank said, his back to me.

"She's what?!" I shouted, but he was already out the door.

Looking back, I see that whether Mimi got pregnant on purpose or not was not the issue. Whether Frank loved me or not was not the issue either. There was little hope for Frank and me then, now or ever, but the fool I was refused to see it.

CHAPTER 14

THE MORNING AFTER THE grievance, though I thought I had gotten it all out of my system, the same old despair was still there. I couldn't seem to make peace with myself over the notion of Caleb getting away with what he did to me. So there was nothing else to do but to present my case to President Cooley. I parked my car in its usual place and walked back to the Administration Building.

It was just before nine. The fall semester hadn't yet started, and campus was quiet and empty. There was a fog, and the University seemed cloaked in soft fur. I could just make out a slight figure coming toward me through the mist, the head looking left, then right. As we came within inches of each other, the figure's startled gaze met mine, and I saw it was Edwin.

"Still protesting in front of the Admin Building?" I asked, coming to a stop on the brick walkway.

"You'll see," he said, without breaking stride. Within a few seconds he was lost in the fog.

I continued on, following the walk until I found myself in front of the Administration Building. The mist half-obscured the courtyard, but there were no voices and no shadows; no evidence of the protest except a broken sign reading "Stop Ap" that loomed up at me out of the fog, impaled in a patch of grass. An imposing figure turned out to be a refuse bin overflowing with paper coffee cups and wrappers. The place was spooky and deserted. But it was early. "You'll see," Edwin had said. With Edwin, that could be anything.

As I entered the lobby, I spotted half a dozen figures hunched into corners like nocturnal animals hiding from the light. From the look of them, they were loiterers, not students, and they seemed to be waiting for something. But I had business to conduct, so I proceeded to the elevator and took it to the fourth floor, where the president's office was located.

On four, the doors opened to a long, white hallway, carpeted in deep pile and lined with elaborately framed portraits of previous presidents as far as the eye could see. I couldn't help but notice they were all middle-aged white guys.

A pair of heavy glass doors etched with "Executive Offices" appeared on my left. I heaved these open to find a small brightly lit lobby and a single receptionist guarding a warren of offices. On her desk, in front of a clutch of painted rocks, stood a brass plaque inscribed with "Carolyn Robinson."

She smiled at me. "How nice to see you, Dr. Braverman."

"I'd like to see the president," I said, getting right to the point.

Carolyn consulted her appointment book. "I don't see anything written here. Did you call to make an appointment?"

"No," I said. "I…I came on impulse."

"I see," Carolyn said, standing up. "I'll just ask if he can squeeze you in." She walked down the hallway and knocked, then stuck her head in. There was a buzz of conversation. A minute later she was back. "Dr. Cooley says to come on in."

I walked down the carpeted hallway and opened that same door. The president was seated behind his desk, a phone to his ear. Cooley was a good-looking man in his mid-fifties, salt and pepper hair framing a wide brow, a face I—60, that is—hadn't seen for fifteen years. He'd left in the late nineties to take retirement in Daytona Beach, then dropped dead of a heart attack the first year he was there. For a dead man, though, he sure looked great.

President Cooley waved me to sit down in one of the two elaborate wing chairs facing the desk. "I'll be with you in a moment," he said.

He swiveled his chair away from me and toward the wall of windows behind the desk, as if he were surveying the little fiefdom that was the University: quads and greens, dormitories and classrooms, parking lots and tennis courts. To his left stood a single glass door leading to a broad balcony behind the windows. I imagined rich old people carrying cocktails onto the balcony to enjoy the view.

I sat there surveying the room. From the looks of things, he must have traveled a lot. Marching around the walls was a series of four Chinese scrolls, the scene evolving from summer to fall to winter to spring. A suit of armor the size of a midget stood at attention in the corner. On the coffee table, one gnarly ginseng root bathed in a liquid inside what looked like a diving bell. Interesting, rich-looking mementos from what no doubt had been an interesting, rich life. Too bad he wouldn't have much of a retirement to enjoy it all.

After several minutes of muffled conversation, Cooley swiveled his chair back. "Now," he said, placing the receiver back on its base. "How can I help you, Margaret?"

"You probably can't do anything about this, but…," I began.

He chuckled as if this were a joke. I guessed everyone must start their supplications that way. "Let's see what it is, first," he said.

"Well, it's…." I said, good and ready to launch into Caleb's unprovoked attack, Joliet's dismissal of the whole thing, the grievance procedure, the sad outcome, the whole story despite the gag order I was supposed to have agreed to. The university president, I rationalized, had to be the one exception to the rule. What interrupted me, though, was a sudden loud noise from the hallway, followed by the receptionist's panicked voice crying, "You can't go in there!"

The president excused himself, crossed the room and opened the door. For a few seconds he just stared before shouting, "What are you doing here?" into the hallway.

More banging. The sound of rattling chains and dragging furniture. I remember wondering whether the ghosts of presidents past had escaped their ornate frames to invade the inner offices. I jumped up and followed Cooley out.

Students were coursing into the foyer, the half dozen loiterers I'd seen in the downstairs lobby and a lot more. As I learned later, eighteen of them had entered the building at different times and from different entrances. Then, at 8:45 a.m. exactly, they'd streamed up the stairs and commandeered the elevators to the fourth floor.

"We're occupying your office to demand divestment!" a short chunky woman in front said. "If you choose to remain in the office, that signals your support for our demands."

In the office there were only the president, Carolyn, and I, and none of us chose to leave. Whether that meant we supported their demands or that we were not going down without a fight was debatable. Meanwhile, the protesters were busy securing the doors with bicycle locks and chains and piling up desks against the doors. A few had run out onto the balcony and were in the process of hanging a banner reading "Apartheid Kills, GU Divest Now." Others were phoning the press and, from the looks of it, their fellow conspirators on the outside. Everyone was bustling about. It looked like a well planned invasion, a siege with Edwin's name all over it.

They roughly pushed us around, shoving the president and me into club chairs. "I don't want to see you move!" the short chunky lady commanded, but generously allowed Carolyn to remain behind her desk. This would turn out to be a mistake that Edwin, had he been there, would never have allowed. But that's what happens when you send a bunch of kids to do a grown-up's job.

As I found out later, a silent alarm had been installed by the administration for just such an occasion. And, according to some prearranged plan, information managed to be passed from President Cooley to the receptionist—a discreet pointed finger by the former and an almost imperceptible nod of acknowledgment from the latter. All Carolyn had to do was to push the button beneath her desk.

The campus police arrived minutes later. They stood outside the foyer doors, staring through the latticework of furniture barricading the glass doors at the demonstrators who were now convening on the floor in a circle, discussing their feelings.

"And you were nervous," I heard one of them say.

"I still am," his neighbor replied.

"Don't worry," the first one said. "Nothing will go wrong."

Oh, the thrill of victory, the warmth of pride; hope for a brand new world; boy, had they put one over on this greedy, lying administration. They had done it, or so they thought.

It turned out, however, that the campus cops were just a decoy: there to divert the protesters' attention while the town police were summoned. Twenty minutes later we heard the crash of glass breaking in the president's office—those lovely windows—and, seconds later, a battalion of bloodstained policemen surged through the door towards us. The students, dragging us with them, retreated to an inner office, some dinky room with no windows and one flimsy door. A familiar-looking boy with acne shoved me down onto the floor. "Aren't you in my Physics 362?" I asked him, but he turned away without answering. I guess I was the enemy.

The demonstrators locked the door and were in the process of barricading it with chairs and desks and boxes and computers, but they ran out of building material. We could hear the police getting ready to bust in the door.

"Do you realize you are committing a felony?" President Cooley asked the short, chunky woman.

Instead of answering, she lifted her arms as if conducting an orchestra. Suddenly, the whole lot of them began to chant over and over, "President Cooley, what's the word? Garriston's not Johannesburg."

They sat there chanting as the police heaved their bodies at the door. One, two, HEAVE! A computer teetered before crashing to the floor. One, two, HEAVE! The door splintered and a pile of boxes cascaded down. One, two, HEAVE! The door came off its hinges, and a dozen police officers armed with guns and clubs lunged through the door. President Cooley, to his credit, told them to hold off, but they weren't listening.

When I remember these were students—babes, really, not criminals—it's clear what followed, but this is from the standpoint of a quarter of a century. The police had no such luxury. To them, the protesters were dangerous felons, ready, if necessary, to torch the building and kill the president. So when the demonstrators all sat down peacefully on the floor and locked arms, the cops didn't see them for the naive idealists they were. Instead of recognizing them as pushovers, duped by a professor with anarchist leanings who set innocent youngsters to do his work for him, the police went berserk, knocking over chairs and computers. They began beating and bloodying the students with their clubs before the president, appalled, finally screamed for them to stop.

It was mayhem, clubs and fists flying. Carolyn and I had backed ourselves into our respective corners, trying to avoid being pummeled to death. All the while the police were dragging the students out, some of them with rivulets of blood dripping from their hairlines down over their faces. Two were unconscious. A couple had broken arms. A pair of the able-bodied demonstrators propped up an injured comrade with their arms under his shoulders as he hopped out of the room, a dazed look on his face. But most were defiant. Those who weren't being dragged feet first swaggered or staggered out, fists in the air and heads held high, ever the revolutionaries. "Stop Apartheid!" they shouted. "End repression!"

I had remembered it all: the violence, the blood, the crack of the police clubs on the kids' heads, computers being tossed like playthings into the wall. But that was just a memory, while this was the real thing. This was

LIFE, vivid and bedazzling: the redness of the blood and the thwack of the clubs, the air crackling with anger and violence and fear. In the past few months, I had lost some of the immediacy I'd felt when I first came back to 1987. I'd begun to take the experience of being here for granted. But suddenly, all over again, I was living it. 35 was holding her arms around herself, shivering with fear, and I was she.

And then we were out. The fog had lifted, and the early September sun was climbing in the sky. Someone threw blankets over Carolyn's and my shoulders, as if we were victims of an accident. President Cooley rejected his, wearing his bloody pin-striped suit as a badge of honor. As one of the campus police walked me to my car, I turned back to see him talking to Janie, of all people. She had her ever-present pad out and was jotting notes at a breakneck pace, the expression on her face that of a predator caught with a juicy piece of meat hanging out of her mouth. I could almost see the blood dribbling down her chin.

I drove myself home, still shaking. I changed out of my clothes and stepped into a hot bath, trying to wash the gore out of my memory. This time, though, I knew it would never wash out.

All of the protesters were arrested, as I remember, and taken to the county jail. Felony charges were filed against all eighteen, and criminal charges against the three leaders. But Edwin was never charged. He'd trained his charges well. Never rat on a colleague, he must have told them, because they never did. Oh, sure, the whole thing—the unfavorable media coverage, the police brutality, the severity of the punishment—served to suck the enthusiasm out of the movement. Everyone was demoralized. Edwin lost his loyal following for the next decade or so, when most of the students abandoned protest entirely. But that was all the comeuppance he got.

I remember asking Edwin several years later what went wrong. He answered me on an abstract level, as if he had never been part of it. It was poorly planned by a small cabal, he said, without the support of large numbers. It was done too early in the morning when a large support protest wasn't possible. They chose a place with so many glass windows that it left them vulnerable. No one expected the administration to call in the police. No one expected the police to be so brutal.

Did he regret that several of the students got kicked out? I asked. Or regret that several paid with jail time? I should have realized, though, that Edwin never had regrets.

"If you're going to talk the talk, you've got to walk the walk," Edwin answered. Then he reminded me that the occupation had worked. After all, the administration divested itself two years later of all its ties to South Africa. "And nobody," he declared, "can say it wasn't a good cause."

Edwin never changed. He waited out the decade or so of apathy and then came back strong against Iraq and Bush the son, commandeered teams of students to help clean up New Orleans in the aftermath of Katrina, and set up a rip-roaring storefront to elect Obama. Good or bad, whatever he wanted he went after, and never got called on the carpet for any of it. Edwin was made of Teflon just as truly as Ronald Reagan ever was. Nothing stuck to him.

There's always some good cause, some just war. Vietnam was the last domino standing against an evil Communist regime, except it wasn't. Iraq had weapons of mass destruction, until it didn't. There's always some old man behind a big desk starting *just* wars, and there are always the young innocents who have to pay for them. So what do I think in all of this? I think the ideal isn't always so ideal. I think the ends don't necessarily justify the means. But life isn't always fair.

CHAPTER 15

THE WAY I REMEMBER it, my disastrous meeting with Mimi came right after Frank and I tried the experiment a third time and failed again. That would have been mid-September—a few weeks from now. Frank, a little irritated, wondered aloud whether I hadn't even tried to fix whatever was wrong; whether I was just out to lure him into that backroom of mine again and hope against hope that we'd end up falling into each other's arms once more. I insisted I had found a couple of inconsistencies and fixed them. He stood up and said it was over. The experiment was a failure and so were we. We argued; we made up; we had great sex on the chair itself, which only added some measure of danger to the erotic mix. Afterwards, we had a heart-to-heart during which he confided that Mimi and he hadn't had sex since the baby was born.

Then Frank left first. I remember sitting there alone, going back over what he had told me, my fury rising. Mimi was such an obsessive, perfectionist bitch. She didn't appreciate him. All she considered was the baby. How dare she marry such a magnificent human being like Frank and then go on to treat him that way. Though he'd never said so much, I was certain that he no longer loved her, maybe that he'd never loved her. But of course he'd never leave her, because of his own stupid moral scruples. He told me once he would never be a deadbeat dad like his father.

Jealous and fuming, I concocted a plan. I would go to Frank's house the following morning, when he was at the university. I'd call Mimi beforehand to make sure she was alone and tell her I knew she was housebound with a little baby and offer her a little adult company. Bring a few danish from Braun's Bakery. Tell her how things stood with Frank and me…. Okay, I didn't really have a clue what I'd say; I'd just have to play it by ear.

That night I tossed and turned, dreaming of disaster, but in the morning I had chased away all my demons and was raring to go. My first class wasn't till early afternoon, so I called around 9:30, after I was sure Frank had left for school. Mimi answered a musical, "hello?" I went through my routine. Would she like a little company, perhaps while the baby slept?

"Of course. That would be very nice," she said in her precise way, the remnants of a slight Chinese sing-song to her voice.

"Eleven?" I asked.

"Eleven," she agreed.

That day is branded into my memory. I dressed simply in pants and the ivory silk blouse Mom had bought me for my thirty-fourth birthday. I went downtown to pick up the danish and, while I was at it, bought a tiny pastel sundress for the little girl and had it wrapped in pink and white paper with a bow.

I remember driving up the circular driveway to their imposing brick colonial home, elegantly landscaped with azaleas, rhododendrons and ringed by tall, stately oak trees. How Frank managed to afford this, I had no idea. I think I heard that Mimi came from old Hong Kong money, her father a high muckety-muck in one of the big banks there.

I parked the Mustang along the side of the drive, and climbed the slate stairs to a heavy wooden door. The door-bell rang chimes. Through the frosted glass side panels I could see her rush down the stairs, probably worrying that the chimes would wake the baby. Mimi opened the door to see me carrying a cake box in one hand and a beribboned gift in the other, her expression somewhere between surprise and amusement.

"Come in," she said, opening the door to a grace-ful foyer. From there we walked into a Martha Stewart-perfect house: tasteful, elegant, immaculate. I thought of Frank with his Madras shirts and mismatched ties and wondered how Mimi ever let him out of the house in such a state. Maybe there was something to that old trope that opposites attract.

I handed her both boxes, and she graciously said thank you, disappearing with the cake box into what I took to be the kitchen. A few minutes later, Mimi was back with a Chinese teapot in the shape of an ornate squash, sever-al matching squash tea cups, and two of my danish, cut into precise quarters, all on a lacquered tray. She waved me to a brocade-covered loveseat nestled between two tables inlaid with mother-of-pearl. "Please, sit," she said.

"Is the baby sleeping?" I asked loudly.

"Yes," she said softly.

"Oh," I whispered back. I've never been very knowledge-able about babies, but I guess I should have realized that noise wakes them up. I felt out of place here. My blonde hair, short and spiky, which had pleased me this morning in the mirror, seemed too edgy now, and my pants, as I sat cross-legged on Mimi's brocade loveseat, rode above the top of my knee-high stockings. My little Mission house with its decorative niches and wood-beamed ceilings all of a sudden seemed gauche and out-of-date, more in line with her husband's Madras shirts and wild ties than with lacquered trays and Chinese tea pots.

"It's so very nice of you to come," Mimi said.

"You've got a lovely home," I replied.

We sat for a half a minute in silence, while she poured out two cups of tea.

"Please," said Mimi, handing me one.

"Thank you," I said. Mimi probably wondered why in heaven I had come. I was beginning to wonder why as well. "Your baby is well?" I asked.

"Wonderful," she said, and took a sip.

We drank in silence for a minute before Mimi added, "I hope you like this tea. It is Dragon Well tea from West Lake, in Hangzhou. Its leaves are a brilliant emerald green, about three-quarters of an inch long and renown throughout China for their beauty."

"Delicious." I reached over and nabbed the closest piece of danish. "The danish are from Braun's Bakery," I said, taking a bite.

Mimi nodded. "Frank likes their cheesecake."

I found myself searching the room for the closest exit. The best route would be to retrace my steps to the front foyer.

"You are a physicist, like my husband, are you not, Dr. Braverman?" Mimi asked.

"Yes. But call me Margaret, please." I wondered whether the mention of her husband qualified as being an opening for what I had come here to say. I decided this was the best opportunity I was ever going to get. "As a matter of fact," I said, "Frank has been helping me with my latest experiment."

"Really?" she said, looking surprised. "What is that?"

I took a deep breath. "Time travel," I answered. "Actually, Frank was integral in helping me to develop a prototype of my time machine."

"Really?" she said again. "I can't imagine Frank being interested in such an outlandish project."

"Maybe you don't know your husband as well as you think," I replied.

Mimi put down her cup and moved forward in her chair. "That sounds very mysterious…what could you possibly mean by that, Dr. Braverman?

"Margaret," I said reflexively. I suddenly realized I didn't know where I was going with this. Should I tell her first about the years of bouncing ideas off one another, the meeting of minds; that eureka moment when we both realized what it all meant? "Well, of course, Frank is a very brilliant man."

"I hardly think you need to tell me that."

"Well, of course, you know that, but perhaps you don't appreciate the originality of his ideas, the true beauty of..."

"Ah," Mimi said, raising her cup and bringing it to her lips. "You are in love with him. Is that what you came here to tell me, Dr. Braverman?"

I resisted the urge to say, "Margaret." It wouldn't matter what she called me now. I suspected that she'd be calling me much worse soon. "Yes," I said. "I came here to tell you that Frank and I are in love," I said.

She gracefully lowered the cup down into its saucer before replying. "Perhaps you are in love with my Frank," Mimi said, emphasizing the "my." "But I highly doubt that he is in love with you."

It was my turn to put her down. "But he is," I assured her. "He told me so."

"During sex, no doubt, when a man will say anything?" Mimi said, her voice turning shrill.

"Yes, during sex, but other times as well. I...."

"You lying bitch," she suddenly cried, standing up.

I guess I knew she'd be angry, but somehow I expected that she'd understand. After all, how can you not have sex with your husband for six months and expect that he won't look elsewhere? "Just ask Frank, if you don't believe me," I said, standing up as well.

"You can go to hell and take him with you!"

"Shhhh. You'll wake the baby," I said.

"Get out of my house!" Mimi screamed, her voice re-sounding off the walls.

At this, there was a loud wail from upstairs. I edged toward the foyer. "Your baby is crying," I said, now running for the front door.

Mimi made no move to go upstairs. Instead, she tore open the front door, and stood there, straight-backed and pursed-lipped, numb to the plaintive crying from upstairs, waiting for me to leave. I hurried out the door to my car and drove home, already wishing that I could go back in time and live that morning over differently.

Of course, going to Mimi's the way I did had reper-cussions. That very evening I got a furious call from Frank asking what I had done. I tried to tell him that I had done it for both our sakes, but my heart wasn't even in it by then.

"Do you know what you've done?" he asked again.

"Yes," I said. "I know what I've done."

"Really?" he asked, his voice crackling with anger. "Do you realize she's thrown me out?"

"Thrown you out?" I asked, thinking maybe this was a good thing.

"Yes, all my clothes, my computer, my books, my files, everything thrown in a pile in front of the house," he shouted. "I tried to talk to her, but she said she'll see me in court."

"I'm sorry. I...."

"I might never see my daughter again! Margaret, how could you do this?"

I could see how I screwed up. I'd thought if we'd just get everything out in the open, we'd all be reasonable and everyone would live happily ever after. Not too bright for a tenured physics professor, I guess. Brilliant but not a jot of common sense, as my mother used to say sometimes when I had done something particularly stupid. "I thought you didn't love her anymore," I said faintly. "I thought you loved me."

There was a deathlike silence on the phone followed at last by a voice so cold it could freeze your soul. "This was the most despicable…I don't ever want to see you again, Margaret," followed by the slam-bang of the phone, then nothing.

It was only a matter of time after Frank's phone call to me that everything fell apart entirely. Not only did Mimi know that Frank and I had been lovers, but she knew that Frank had been my partner in the time travel experiment. This was her ace in the hole. Fueled by the fury that can only come from a woman scorned, she marched to the *Garriston News* office and told Janie Carr everything she knew.

I expect Janie listened with glee, picturing how this would be the climax to her lurid time travel series expose. In any case, it must have been rushed into print, because there was "**Mysterious Stranger in Time Travel Lab revealed!**" in bold at the top of the first page of that afternoon's edition of the *Garriston News*. I remember the article practically word for word:

> *An unexpected development occurred yesterday afternoon when an elegant lady carrying a baby entered the news office, asking for this reporter. She introduced herself as Mimi Mermonstein, the wife of physics professor Frank Mermonstein, whom she identified positively as being the 'mysterious assistant' in Dr. Margaret Braverman's time travel experiment.*
>
> *Ms. Mermonstein related how she had just come from a meeting with Dr. Braverman, who had confessed to her that Frank had been the one helping her in her lab. When asked why she was telling me this, she said that she felt it was her public duty to tell the University that her husband had been secretly involved in a dangerous experiment that had already threatened the integrity of the science building. Ms. Mermonstein also stated that because time travel can in no way be possible, to endanger innocent lives with such a ludicrous experiment is unforgivable. She fully expects the*

*Physics Department to take steps
to punish the offenders.*

Dr. Joliet had been diagnosed by now and was not looking at all well when he called the departmental meeting to order early in the fall semester. After a few moments of getting rid of old business, in obvious pain, he asked Caleb, as vice chairman, to take over.

Most of the rest of us showed our concern for the poor old guy, but not Caleb. His face was suffused with—what can I even call it?—the power of the position. I think it was Henry Kissinger who said that academic politics is so vicious precisely because the stakes are so small. There's no big money here, at least if you don't have a PBS series. There aren't a lot of perks unless you have relatives who want a college education at a discount. In the end, there's not a lot to fight for except an office with a window or a title on a door. We're supposed to be above it all—with our thoughts on abstractions and moral imperatives. But we're not. I've seen academics fighting tooth and nail over a reserved parking space. The stakes are truly that small.

So I wasn't surprised to see Caleb's eyes light up at the prospect of wielding power over the rest of us. He conducted the rest of the meeting, his voice lower by an octave, his enunciation crisper, his posture straighter. And by the time he reached the real piece of business: that is, accusing the two of us of deception and breach of conduct, he had managed to attain a kind of Lawrence Olivier majesty in tone and manner.

Brandishing the *Garriston News* article of two days before, Caleb read, in orotund tones:

"*...Mimi Mermonstein, the wife of physics professor Frank Mermonstein, whom she identified positively as being the 'mysterious assistant' in Dr. Margaret Braverman's time travel experiment.*"

"That's not a complete sentence," I couldn't help but call out—anything to throw him off his game. A few people tittered, but Caleb would have none of it.

"Please don't interrupt, Margaret," Caleb chided. "You're already in enough trouble as it is."

"Yessir, Caleb, sir," I said.

He gave me a scolding look. "Both of you have lied to this department. You've put university property at risk. Margaret, I'm going to have to recommend that for this coming year you are put on probation. If you so much as go into that back lab of yours, tenure or no tenure, I'm going to see that you are brought up on charges."

You know, after the grievance hearing, I had thought seriously about pursuing an appeal. In 2012 this would have been relatively easy. I could have applied to the Federal Office of Civil Rights and might actually have gotten a favorable decision. But in 1987, the buck stopped at the Grievance Committee. And once there was a decision, it stayed confidential. Sure, the grievant could take the risky step of leaking the meeting contents, but then she'd have to be prepared to pay the consequences. Most likely she would have been branded a traitor and condemned for slandering a colleague. So a lot of us kept quiet.

But there was always that option, I remember thinking, and Caleb had to know that. I had that little piece of dirt on him, and if he strayed just the tiniest bit too far, I might be tempted to use it against him. Besides, I did have tenure, after all.

"Ooh, I'm afraid," I said, not afraid at all.

Caleb gave me one long glare before turning his magisterial gaze toward the far side of the table. "And, you, Frank," Caleb said. "In light of this breach of conduct, I'm going to have to recommend against your upcoming tenure."

I had forgotten how low Caleb could go. Unwilling to hit me directly, he would get back at me by denying Frank tenure, something that he had always dreamed of doing, anyway.

Frank, in his accustomed seat at the back of the room, in wrinkled jeans and shirt, the result no doubt of living out of a suitcase in Motel 6 just outside town, shook his head in disbelief.

I still wasn't worried, though. The rest of the department, independent thinkers, or so I thought, would never take this lying down.

But, no. A lot of heads nodded. The traitors!

"Any questions, comments before we vote?" Caleb dared them.

Henri made a half-hearted attempt at defending Frank

and me. He'd heard we defended him in his own absence. Mark protested that we were drumming out of the department two of the most talented physicists we had. Edwin maintained that Frank was innocent until proven guilty, and refusing him tenure without proof of guilt was denying him his rights.

"Dr. Joliet," I cried, against the encroaching silence. "You don't have to go along with this. Take the meeting back. You're still the chairman."

But Dr. Joliet, his attention wholly captured by something out the window, said nothing.

Not a word from anybody. I almost found myself agreeing with Caleb when, a handful of meetings ago, he complained that, "none of you wusses say a thing."

"Let's vote," Caleb said this time.

By a slight majority, the censure held.

Three weeks later, when the tenure committee met, they rubber-stamped the whole thing. Frank could finish out the year. He might even be hired for the following year, but his tenure was denied. Frank didn't even wait to find out whether he'd be rehired. Disgusted, he gave in his notice, and the day after Commencement, Frank left for good.

Anyway, that is how I remembered the whole thing happening the first time I lived it. It remained to be seen how it would play out this time.

CHAPTER 16

Sᴇᴘᴛᴇᴍʙᴇʀ 15: ʟɪᴠɪɴɢ ᴛʜʀᴏᴜɢʜ it a second time. I was already inside the lab when Frank entered, looking over his shoulder. "No sign of the reporter," he said as he closed the door and locked it behind him.

I had the backroom door open and was already standing inside the threshold. "It's ready to go," I said.

I think we were both on edge on our third attempt, trying to evade Janie Carr and clinging to the hope that three times is a charm. We certainly wasted no words.

"Let's get this thing over with," Frank replied, crossing the floor to where I was standing. "I promised Mimi I'd be back by dinnertime."

I sat down on the chair and Frank set the timing mechanism. "Ready?" he asked.

"Ready," I said, my voice a little muffled in the helmet. This time it would work, I knew 35 was thinking. I closed my eyes tight.

Frank pushed the button.

Nothing.

It was no surprise for me, of course: I'd had twenty-five years to mull it over, but 35 was devastated. I remember thinking that this was the end of my dream. It took a couple of minutes before I managed to push off the helmet.

"Success?" Frank asked.

I shook my head, no.

You could see him deflate. "Damn it, Margaret. Did you even try to fix whatever was wrong?"

35 was just as incensed. "What the hell, Frank? I told you I found a few logical inconsistencies in the wiring and fixed them. Nothing else was wrong."

"*Obviously*, there is something wrong," Frank said with elaborate sarcasm. "Did it ever occur to you, Margaret, that maybe in 2012 you don't want this to happen? That you simply don't put on the helmet at the time you're supposed to?" He paused for effect. "Or that you're dead?"

It had occurred to me, of course, many times through the years, but back then I simply closed my mind to it. Either alternative—that I was so dead inside as to give up on the whole thing, or that I was simply dead—was inconceivable.

"Now you're being mean," was the best I could do.

"And sometimes," Frank said, ignoring me, "I wonder whether you aren't just out to lure me into this backroom of yours in the hope that we'll end up falling into each other's arms again."

I could feel the fury seething through my body. "You think that the experiment is nothing but a smokescreen for getting you into bed?" I shot back. "If that's all you think of me, you can just get out!"

Frank glared at me. "That's exactly what I'm going to do! The experiment is a failure and so are we." He turned to go.

I let him get half way across the floor of the front room before I called him back.

"Don't leave, Frank," I pleaded.

"Why, Margaret?" he said, turning around. "Why won't you let me go?"

That was the problem, of course. I wouldn't let him go. And somehow Frank couldn't break the tie until I gave it up. We stared at each other for a few moments, first with the remnants of anger, then with a growing hunger neither of us could seem to help.

"I *did* fix it," I said, tears running down my cheeks. "I really did. I wasn't just trying to get you to make love to me." That's debatable, I said to myself, but it didn't matter what I thought. 35 believed it.

Frank had started the long walk back. We met in the threshold.

"I'm sorry," he said, enveloping me in his arms.

"So am I," I answered, my mouth already on his lower lip, sucking it into my mouth.

We collapsed onto the chair, the only soft place in the room. Frank pushed up the helmet as I loosened his belt. He kissed my neck, his mouth descending down into my blouse, as he undid the buttons one by one, then further as he undid the zipper on my pants, then diving deeper as he tore apart the lacy underpants I had chosen for this very occasion. I could feel him grow hard against me as his mouth reached my crotch, his tongue exploring the soft nooks and crannies of me until, all of a sudden, he turned me over. My pants around my knees, he entered me from the back, with each thrust, the chair bucking like an animal. Maybe it was a measure of danger that added to the erotic mix: some fearful fancy that we might set it off by our passion, catapulting the two of us into the void where nothing existed but us. And perhaps the magic worked, because for some timeless interval, there was no light or dark, no good or bad, no high or low, no after or before, no way to define either of us except by way of each other.

Lying there on the chair afterwards, my head nestled in a bed of curly hair on his chest, I couldn't help but think, remember this! Remember the warmth of his skin, his unique sweaty aroma, the love given and returned. Remember the tangibility of it, the realness. Remember this, because this is the last time. Whether I succeed in changing anything or not, this will be the very last time.

We lay there for another ten or fifteen minutes in that position, rambling on about this or that, nothing important, until Frank began to talk about Mimi. How he remembered, at the beginning, before they knew each other very well, that he'd been struck by the lilt in her voice, her elegance, her passion. How they got involved, he couldn't remember quite how, but all of a sudden she was pregnant and she insisted it was his. And how different it had been since their daughter was born, how it was always the baby who came first. The child slept between them, and Mimi insisted sexual intercourse would leave traumatic memories in her developing psyche. How they hadn't had sex since the baby was born.

What I hadn't remembered was that this led into another long tangent: how his father had gone out for a pack of cigarettes when he was five and never came back. His mother had been absolutely devastated and blamed herself. If only she had been more cheerful, a better cook, a better lover. She went to work at a hair salon, which was the only thing she knew how to do, and the two of them moved from apartment to apartment every time they couldn't pay the rent. How for years he had tried to be the perfect son, because with all her problems, he never wanted to add to her grief.

What Frank was telling me was that no matter how bad his marriage was, he would never be the one to leave. Funny how I never recalled this part. In all the years I'd thought back to this, all I'd remembered was that Mimi was a bitch who withheld sex.

Then Frank left first, as he had before. Everything that had happened today was exactly the way it had that first time. But for me—60—I knew this was a turning point. Suddenly I understood him. Frank would never leave his family in the lurch. Going to see Mimi to tell her that the two of us were in love, and expecting that miraculously Frank and I would be free to come together was a fool's errand. No matter how I played it, it would never happen. All I'd accomplish would be to ruin all of our lives. I had to stop myself from carrying out what I was about to do.

CHAPTER 17

TIME IS NOT ABSOLUTE. Einstein proved that a century ago. It is relative, even subjective. Each of us generates our own timeline in the very living of it. It's not exactly the same as anyone else's, even if, like sex or the latest, hottest film, we experience it together. We cannot share our experiences, because they are our own. No one can know what goes on in someone else's head. All we can do is to view the same movie and laugh together as we watch, or cry out in ecstasy at the very moment that your lover does the same. Every one of us generates her own experience and with it her own time. It makes for a lonelier existence, but one hopefully where we are responsible for our own actions.

I had to tell myself this as 9:30 rolled around. I knew just what 35 was thinking. Frank must have left for school by now, and there would be time to go through the confession, the heart to heart, and leave, if not on good terms, at least on pragmatic ones. I knew what 35 was thinking, because I had been there. But that way disaster lay.

Mimi answered that same musical, "hello?" I went through my routine, unaltered from the last time. Would she like a little company, perhaps while the baby slept?

"Of course that would be very nice."

"Eleven?"

"Eleven."

I tried, even then, to change the routine, to say something else, but all I had under my control were three fingers on my right hand and two on the left. My mouth, apparently, was not part of the deal.

So, anxious as I was, I had no choice but to go along with the plot. I showered and put on my pants and the ivory silk blouse. At one point, I tried pulling out a skirt just to change the equation, but pants it turned out to be. Try as I might, I could not seem to commit a single new act. The idea came to me, though, that even if I could not do anything new, perhaps I could stop myself from doing something I had done before. I went downtown to buy the danish and tried hard not to enter Jan's Baby House, but my feet took me there nevertheless. Only with great concentration did I manage to pass up the pastel sundress and to replace it, still wrapped in the same pink and white paper with a bow, with a terry romper. That single insignificant variation, while not much, I exulted, might be just enough to set the whole day on a different path.

It was ten forty by the time I got back into my Mustang, placing the cake and gift on the passenger's seat. I started the motor and set off, a trip of about twenty minutes. On the way, my hands on the steering wheel, I flexed my pinky finger on the right hand, then the ring finger, then the middle one. Then I concentrated all my focus on the index finger, imagining that it would tap the steering wheel, and it did! I imagined my right thumb doing the same, and it did! I felt a tingle of fear as 35 startled at the runaway hand, and decided that would have to do for now. Any more might give away the element of surprise.

The car made its own way past palatial mansions amidst old growth oaks and maple trees to Mimi's house. There, through the leaves, I could just make out the brick colonial home, edged by azaleas and rhododendrons and fronted by a circular driveway. As the Mustang's signal light blinked right, I—60—grabbed the wheel with both hands and swerved left, past the driveway, holding on for dear life with every one of my ten fingers, ignoring as best I could the feel of a fight-or-flight adrenalin rush of terror in my body, and the pull of antagonist muscles bent on breaking the rebel hold on the wheel. I can only imagine what 35 must have felt—that some phantom had taken hold of her hands—or maybe that she'd just gone stark raving mad. But I couldn't help any of that. I couldn't let her determine things anymore. What had happened the first time was not going to happen again. As much as I disliked Mimi, I wasn't going to break up their home. That much I could choose myself. And if that meant that she didn't inform on her husband to Janie, and consequently, that Frank never left academia, I would peacefully –happily!—accept whatever fate had in store for me back in 2012.

I struggled the rest of the way to the university. By now 35 had gone into some sort of shock, and it was possible to override her, steering my legs toward the seventh floor lab. To someone watching me from the campus green or from above, through the big windows of an upper story lab, I must have looked drunk or disabled. My right leg was completely under my control, but the left one tended to drag behind. At one point I was forced to grab it with my left hand to move it forward. It took me almost half an hour to get from the parking lot to the science building. A stack of *Garriston News* stood by the elevator. I picked one up as I waited for the doors to open.

The headline said, "**Physics Professor caught in the act!**" Oh, no, I thought. What had I done now?

The doors opened to an empty elevator. I entered, reading:

> This morning police officers escorted Dr. Caleb Winter to the Garristontown Police Station. Dr. Winter, a member of the physics faculty, was charged with lewd behavior to sophomore, Tammy Briggs, in his office last evening.
>
> Tammy, sobbing, her sweater torn, ran to the first security officer she found, Officer Michael Hanley. She had no business in Dr. Winter's office, she told him, but as she returned from trying to see Dr. Braverman, her professor in particle physics, "he lured me into his office. When I tried to leave, he grabbed me, ripping my sweater." Dr. Winter was without comment.

I was laughing as I entered the lab, though I can't say who found it funniest, 35 or me. The wall clock in the front room said one fifteen; my class started in fifteen minutes, but I had no more motivation to teach today. I picked up the phone and called the department secretary, asking her to please put a note on the door of the class saying that something had come up and class was dismissed for the day. The kids would certainly have no problem with that.

Then I unlocked the door to the backroom. 35 was still fighting to regain control of what she clearly thought of as her body. I smiled to myself at the image of 35 discovering herself in the helmet seconds after I had left. Trying out her newfound powers over her own body. Her look of relief, of confusion, of dawning comprehension…. Well, she could have it all to herself in a few minutes. There was something urgent I had to do first: return myself to 2012.

I walked over to the machine and set the mechanism two minutes back from its original setting: 5:01 on May 3, 2012. I'd long since figured out why the thing didn't work, but until now I couldn't do anything about it. Clearly, I'd sabotaged the helmet the moment I got back, anytime before 5:03. So, the reason neither of those two last attempts had succeeded wasn't that there was anything wrong. Nothing WAS wrong. The concept WAS sound, as I'd claimed. As long as I got back sometime between 5:00, when I left the first time, and 5:03 when the helmet was destroyed, it would be free sailing.

I sat down in the chair and pulled the helmet down

over my head, one last time beholding the lab at the way it used to be: shiny and new, the sound of jackhammers and electric saws filling the air. "Thanks," I said aloud with my thirty-something lips. "It was great to be back." I reached around the back to the small black button and pressed.

There was the whoosh of disembodiment, that indescribable sensation of Me filling the entire universe, which, once you got the hang of it, wasn't exactly unpleasant. And then I was back, though it took me a half a minute to get my wits about me. I lifted my eyes to the digital readout, which said 5:02. Only then did I rip off the helmet and furiously tear out SQUID modules, throwing them every which way, until the clock said 5:03. Then I decided it must have been enough, because I had no 35-year-old alter ego in my head, as far as I could tell. Then again, I doubted that I would tell the difference unless some part of me—my right pinky finger, for example—decided to start moving against my will.

As for destroying my invention, really, we were both better off without it. Sure, posterity would never know of my greatest accomplishment, but I did, and somehow that was enough for me now.

I locked the door to the backroom behind me and crossed the floor of the lab, past the retrocausality set-up with its lasers, prisms, splitters, and miles of coiled-up fiber-optic cable. The place looked a little dowdy after twenty-five years, but at least there were no jackhammers splitting the air. I went out the door and down seven floors to the lobby, my knees clicking and aching the way they used to, and out to the back parking lot. The sun, a big bright orb about fifteen degrees above the horizon, hadn't gone down yet; and the night was hot for May; well, maybe hot for 1987 if not for 2012. The trees had long since shed their blossoms, and the spring flowers gone as if they never existed. The network of lights weren't set to turn on for an hour or two. Everything looked exactly as if I had never left.

I found my Honda in the usual place. I unlocked the door and got in, started the motor and headed to the exit. Most of the remaining students were hunkered down, I suspected, doing last-minute papers, but the few I saw looked normal, if strange by the standards of a quarter of a century ago. There were no more broad-shouldered jackets and big hair, but I didn't miss them in the least. I passed a tall young man in cargo shorts and flip-flops, an iPhone to his ear, and smiled to myself.

On my right, Bed, Bath and Beyond, Kohl's and Best Buy went by, Braun's Bakery and Vinnie's Shoe Repair, the stuff of memory. I drove on through the streets till I reached my own house: a little worse for wear perhaps but still standing. I pulled into the driveway and shut off the motor, so excited to come home that I didn't even bother to open the garage. I climbed the brick stairs to the front door. Inside, I could see the lights on. I'd done that a lot lately, leaving the lights on. I must be getting old, I thought. I turned the key in the lock and went in to the same arched windows and plastered ceilings with their exposed wooden beams.

But something was amiss. The dusty old tables, the *tchotchkas* in their decorative niches—all gone, and in their place, a light-colored modular set; a glass table, a potted plant. In the air I sniffed the unmistakable smell of chili, plus some other things I couldn't identify. I followed the aromas to the kitchen.

"Hi, sweetie," I heard as I rounded the corner.

And there he was, twenty-five years older, of course, his hair a mass of silver, his middle a little thicker and the chest a little broader, but with the same strong jaw line and the sharp slope of the cheekbones. He was wearing an apron, and stirring a big pot on the stove. He leaned over, threw his sticky hand around my neck and kissed me smack on the mouth. "What's new?" he asked.

I couldn't help but lean against the wall to regain my equilibrium. My mouth seemed frozen, and if I didn't sit down, I would fall down. I moved, as smoothly as I could, my hands braced against the wall the whole way, over to a little café chair, part of a set of two around a tiny wrought iron table, neither of which was there the last time I'd looked. I dropped down. "Tired," I said.

Frank was busy stirring the chili, his back to me. "Oh, by the way, Marge, you remember, don't you, that Morgan's coming to dinner?"

I swallowed. "Morgan?" I said. "You mean my lab assistant?"

He turned toward me, noticing how white I was. "You feeling all right?" he asked, putting a hairy arm up to my forehead. "Cool," he said, shrugging his shoulders. "No, not your lab assistant. I didn't even know you had a lab assistant named Morgan. No, Morgan, my daughter. She's in town for that genetics conference." He gave me one more long look before turning back to the stove.

I sat there silent, brooding. The present felt like a house built on a sand foundation. This 2012 couldn't be trusted: it must be some alternate reality, one potential universe in an infinite multiverse. It might disappear in a puff of smoke or a whoosh of disembodiment. I wanted to believe it, but it was all too much to take in. How did I end up with Frank? Not an hour ago in 1987, I had deliberately *not* wrecked his marriage to Mimi. How did this happen? And how was I going to find out? To ask was to challenge the reality of the last twenty-five years, something I was terrified of doing for fear of changing it all back again.

Let's see. I had disassembled the helmet. The last thing Frank would have remembered, if 1987 were indeed the way I last left it, was that the experiment failed. It blew up first and then never worked at all. Would it shock him to know that it had? That I had changed his very life without him knowing? But time is not absolute, I couldn't help thinking. Each person's time is subtly different from anyone else's. How could I, in changing my life, change Frank's life, too?

This was all too much for me. "I need a drink," I said,

steadying myself on the wrought iron table as I ratcheted my body into a standing position. Damn, it had been nice being thirty-five again. I stumbled into the hallway to the old built-in cabinet I kept the liquor in. Thankfully, it was still there. I pulled out the bottle of Jack Daniels and carried it back into the kitchen, where I went to get a glass from the cabinet over the microwave, which had mysteriously morphed into a convection oven. Never mind. I opened the cabinet to find…cups. No matter. I pulled out a cup, filled it with ice from the freezer, which was fortunately still in the same place, and poured myself a stiff drink.

"Thought you didn't drink that stuff anymore, Marge," Frank said, looking at me a little strangely. "I opened one of the new bottles of pinot noir we bought last month." He gestured to the bottle on the island.

Here I'd changed his whole life without his knowing it; yet Frank was the one completely at home with the present reality. It was I who didn't know my way around. "I need something a little stronger," I said, sitting down again.

The doorbell rang.

"That'd be Morgan," Frank said, turning his head to look at me. "Would you get it, Marge?"

"Sure," I said, my heart pounding. Strange to think why I should be so terrified to see the grad student I had last seen a few hours ago. I stood up and made my way down the hallway to the front door. Through the peep hole I could see someone who looked just like the Morgan Wong

I knew but with a better haircut. I opened the door.

Morgan came into the foyer with a broad smile and a cake box. "Margaret!" she said. I couldn't help but think she was being a little informal. She'd always called me Dr. Braverman.

"It's been a long time!" she said as she gave me a hug.

"How long has it been?" I asked. Now that I looked at her, I could see Mimi in the eyes and hair; but it was Frank from the mouth down.

Morgan looked at me, her brow wrinkled, the way it always did when she was puzzled. "Three months ago. I came for Dad's birthday party. You remember."

"Of course. Dad's birthday party."

"I smell Dad's chili," she said, sniffing.

"Yup. Come on in," I said, taking a long slug from my cup. "He's in the kitchen."

"That the latest style—drinking hard liquor from a cup?" she asked.

"How's your mother?" I asked instead.

Morgan looked a little surprised at the question. "Still in Milwaukee. Okay, I think. I haven't seen her in awhile."

"I don't remember. What's her new husband's name?"

She looked even more surprised. "Peter. And they've been married since 1990, the year before you and Dad got married. Margaret, are you all right?"

I decided I'd better stop asking questions for awhile. "Sure," I said, taking another slug from the cup. "Just a senior moment, I guess."

By now we had made it to the kitchen, where Morgan put down the cake box, kissed her father on his nose and sampled chili from the large wooden spoon he held out. It all seemed so natural, so inevitable. Morgan, my grad assistant, who hadn't seen her father since she was a baby, damaged from a broken family, clearly belonged to some other universe, the same one with her man-hating mother who had never married again.

In that other universe, Morgan, the product of a brilliant father and a meticulous mother, must have planned the whole thing out. She found out from Mimi about Frank's affair and how she had thrown him out of the house. For twenty years, her mother raged about how much she hated that man. Surely Morgan would be curious about who the other woman was who had wrecked her parents' marriage. It certainly wouldn't have been hard to Google Margaret Braverman on the Internet. So Morgan made up some story about hearing great things about my reputation and entreated me to be her thesis advisor.

And somewhere along the line she discovered the backroom and the time machine. She didn't tell anyone. She just went about urging a sad old spinster to go back to change the past. How hard could that have been? "What I wouldn't give to go back and do things differently," I remember saying. How strangely Morgan had looked at me then. "Maybe you should," she replied.

But I'd never know any of this for sure because in this particular universe, the one where Frank and I were a couple, and Morgan herself was in genetics, not physics, none of that had happened.

Morgan and I set out the plates and silverware on the heavy trestle table in the dining room, the only piece of furniture left from that alternate reality. The three of us sat at one end and ate chili and salad and French bread and talked about Morgan's appointment as assistant professor of genetics at a small college in New England; her husband of two years, Ralph; Frank's latest research on the theory of everything.

"How's *your* research going?" Morgan asked me, at last.

I didn't know what to say. The lab hadn't seemed to be any different when last I'd looked. Wasn't it the same retrocausality experiment I saw on the table? I no longer could be sure of anything.

"Oh, Margaret hardly has time to do research any more. She's in such demand to demonstrate her new machine," Frank said.

It was all I could do to stop from asking what infernal new machine he was talking about. Fortunately, Morgan spoke before I did. "You mean the Superconducting Quantum Interference Device?" she asked.

I upended my glass and took a good, long slug. It took so long that Frank answered in my place.

"The SQUID, of course!" Frank enthused. "Ever since Margaret converted that failed time machine of hers into a device for recording brain waves in real time, the world has beaten a path to her door. They're still finding new uses for it."

I swallowed hard.

"Like?" Morgan asked.

Frank looked to me, but I had already picked up the bottle and begun to pour another glass. "Go on," I said, smiling at him. "You're doing such a good job."

"Well, the newest is analyzing the progression of brain disease, like Alzheimer's," he said, taking the bottle from me and pouring another glass for Morgan and one for himself. "The helmet's easy to use, compact, noninvasive, and produces incredibly precise images. Not to mention that it works at room temperature. Just fit the helmet to the head, and you've got a wealth of data."

Morgan looked impressed. "How did you ever think to convert that silly helmet to such a wonderful use, Margaret?"

Normally I would have taken offense at the term *silly helmet*, but I was too far gone with all the wine and the weirdness. Besides, I was wondering myself how I'd done it. I figured I must have used quantum tunneling through an insulating barrier resulting in a superconducting loop— exactly the same as before, but with a different application. I'd have to get my hands on one of the devices and reverse engineer it to be sure.

"Unfortunately, my dear, it's a trade secret," I said, instead. "If I told you, I'd have to kill you." We all laughed, and I figured that that took care of that.

"Actually," Frank said after we had stopped laughing, "I always wondered why you gave up on the idea of time travel so abruptly."

The question hung in the air. I figured someone had to answer it.

"I don't know," I ended up saying. "I guess I figured that it was a bad idea in the first place. Can you imagine what would have happened if it had worked? Once the world got a hold of it, everyone would be zooming back and forth in time. It would destabilize everything."

"What a thought," Morgan remarked, shuddering.

"At the time," Frank said, "I thought it was just sour grapes. You know, Marge, how you never could deal with failure."

"Well, I don't know about that!" I huffed, but Frank was still talking.

"I remember telling you not long after Mimi left me that I was free to help again. I even offered to transport myself, to do whatever worked, but you just looked at me in horror." He frowned at the memory. "And *then* you told me you'd destroy it before you'd let me mess up what you'd just fixed."

"Fixed what?" Morgan chimed in, looking at me.

Wow, I thought. Did I really say that? How could 35 have even known that anything got fixed? I glanced up to see Morgan, her brow furrowed, still waiting for an answer.

"Well, I don't even remember that," I answered back. "But maybe what I meant was that I had just fixed my life. Finally gotten time travel out of my system."

Morgan seemed satisfied.

"Anyway, by then," I added, hoping I was right, "I had

already started transforming it into the SQUID."

"Probably so," said Frank, shrugging.

We finished the pinot noir that Frank and I had supposedly bought a case of and started another. I made a pot of coffee and went to cut the strings on the cake box. Inside, there were four cheese danish. I cut them in quarters, put them on a large plate my mother had left me and brought them out. I suddenly wondered what happened to the four cheese danish I'd gotten for Mimi the second time around but never got around to giving her. I must have left them in the passenger seat of the Mustang, back in 1987. 35 must have found them that evening and eaten them herself. Or given them to Frank. I had no idea what happened because I wasn't there. I'd skipped twenty-five years of what was ostensibly a wonderful life that I'd never know. But I didn't care. I was only grateful that this was my reality now.

And yet....I had to know something. Could I possibly have changed anyone else's life as well? Ruined it, even, in my mad rush through time?

"I wonder whatever happened to Caleb Winter," I asked, as if reminiscing.

"Wow. Caleb. Does that bring back memories," Frank said, stacking Morgan's plate on top of his, and mine on top of hers.

"Caleb?" Morgan said. "I don't think I ever heard of him."

"He was in the Physics Department years ago, Sweetie," Frank said. "He got kicked out after he tried to rape a student. Not that I ever liked him much, but it totally ruined his career. The last I heard I think he was in New Zealand doing something with sheep." He shook his head. "Whatever made you think of Caleb?"

"Just came to mind," I said. "Frank, who's the chairman of the Physics Department?"

"Who's the chairman of the Physics Department?" Frank repeated, staring at me. "Are you all right, Marge?"

"I'm fine. Just bear with me for a second. Who is it?"

"Walter, of course. For the past fifteen years." He made a move to feel my head again, but I swerved.

"Yeah," Morgan said. "When I first came in, she asked me what was the name of Mimi's new husband."

"New husband?" Frank said. "What new husband? What happened to Peter?"

"No," Morgan said. "I just mean…."

"And Edwin?" I broke in. "What's he doing?"

"This is scaring me, Marge," Morgan said.

"I promise I'll tell you everything when we're done. Edwin?" I prompted.

Frank shrugged. "Same old, same old. He's still bugging everyone to show up next Tuesday for the Occupy Movement teach-in."

I smiled. Same old Edwin, Thank God. I hadn't really wanted anything to burst his bubble. I upended my wine glass before asking the big one. "And Mark?"

"Well," Frank said. "You know Mark. He doesn't tell me a whole lot…."

Then he's still alive, at least.

"But Jerry tells me he's okay...." Frank went on.

Thank God he's okay. I had the most awful foreboding that he was....Jerry? "Jerry's alive!?" I couldn't help but screech.

Frank looked at me with concern. "Oh, Marge. You've lost your memory, haven't you? When did this happen? This morning you seemed fine."

I smiled. This morning I was a sad, lonely spinster, not fine at all. I leaned over and planted my lips on his in a long kiss, the sweetness of the wine intermingling with the taste of joy.

"Believe me. I am so fine," I said. "You can't believe how fine I am."

Frank smiled back. "I hope so," he said.

"So what does Jerry tell you?" I asked.

"That Mark's in the hospital," he said. "He didn't want anyone to know about it."

So like Mark. But what if my mucking around with time had somehow made his condition more serious?

"He said Mark's having his hump removed," Frank was saying. "It made him very self-conscious."

I couldn't help but laugh. "But the two of them still have AIDS?" I asked.

"Marge, I...."

"Just this one last thing."

"Yes, of course, they still have AIDS. There's no cure."

Damn, I thought. I wouldn't have minded changing that.

"Margaret?" Morgan said. "You want to tell us what's going on?"

"Okay, but first some sustenance." I reached over the table to pour what was left of the bottle into our three glasses. I was just lifting the glass to my lips when my right pinky finger rose of its own accord and made a little circle in the air.

CHAPTER 18

Ⅰ ENDED UP GIVING FRANK and Morgan the abridged version: enough to allay their worries but not enough to actually bring them up to the minute. In other words, I said nothing about the fact that 35 had somehow managed to make the trip as well.

I wondered how that had happened. Had I transported the two of us at once? Or more likely, had she figured the whole thing out in that last hour in 1987 as I was hijacking the car and dragging her from pillar to post?

Yes, that had to be it. 35 was me. She was in shock, to be sure, but she wasn't unconscious and she was smart. Of course she'd figured the whole thing out: that I'd come from the future; that the helmet worked; that it had always worked. And then, with an intuition that can only come of knowing what she herself would do under the circumstances, followed me back within the half minute before I came to my senses and tore the damn thing to pieces.

I figured this all out the night after Morgan left and Frank and I had made love—exhilarated, mindboggling love—love, for me, at least, that hadn't happened to this body for twenty-five years—and fallen into bed in a state of total exhaustion. But I couldn't sleep. I got up, went downstairs, poured myself another cup of Jack Daniels and put my feet up on the new glass coffee table.

You try to fix one thing and end up screwing up another, I mused. By going back in time, I'd gotten back together with Frank. But by returning home, I'd disclosed to 35 that the helmet worked. The whole conundrum reminded me of the Taoist yin-yang symbol—the circle which contains two teardrop-shaped halves, one white and one black, neither able to exist without its complement, each giving rise to the other. Every quality contains the germ of its own opposite, each object the seeds of its own destruction.

I upended the last drops of whiskey into my mouth.

The only conceivable course was to return 35 to 1987. After all, how could she live out all those years if she were here in 2012 with me? And how could I be alive now if I didn't exist before?

Anyway, all this lofty speculation wouldn't even buy a cup of coffee. The fact was that I simply couldn't stand knowing she was in my head for the rest of my life. No, I couldn't live like that—35 watching my every move, 35 judging me just as I judged her. No, she had to go back, whether she wanted to or not.

◊

THE FOLLOWING MORNING I tried to follow the routine that Frank and I had apparently been engaging in for the past twenty-something years. Frank made the coffee and sliced the fruit. I made the oatmeal and the toast. We sat down at the little wrought iron table and chairs, our iPads precariously poised behind our plates and open to the New York Times. We walked down the stairs to the garage where we kissed before driving off in the same direction but in separate cars. Nothing exciting, but deeply wonderful when compared to the alternative.

I'd checked my schedule to confirm that my first class was not till eleven. There would be plenty of time to go to the lab and return my counterpart to 1987. Of course, I would have to fill her in on what I was doing before I did it. The problem was that 35 and I were two solitudes within a single head: neither of us could hear the other.

I figured when I got there, I'd open up my iPad and write directly on the screen. She'd read what I had to say, and maybe, if I relaxed my fingers, she'd be able to write back. We'd come to some amicable agreement, such as not publishing what she had found, and she'd be off to her life and I to mine. That was the plan.

I drove my Honda to the back parking lot and walked myself into the science building. I unlocked the door to the lab. No one was there and everything seemed unchanged; the same experiment set-up sat on the main table. The door to the backroom was locked, as I had left it the night before. I placed my iPad on the nearest table and unlocked the door.

Inside, the helmet was lying askew on the floor, its insides spilling out, SQUID modules sprinkled like lumps of sugar on a birthday cake. I closed the door behind me before gathering them up one by one. Then I sat down in the chair and proceeded to methodically fit them back into the helmet.

When I had the helmet back together, I placed it carefully back on the pole, opened the door and sat down at the table with the iPad in front of me. I lifted the cover, opened a new window on the screen and began to type.

"You've got to go back," I wrote. "There's nothing to be changed here. Everything is perfect."

I let my hands relax on the keyboard. First the right pinky flexed, then the right ring finger. Then the other fingers of the right hand, in sequence, and finally each one of the left. She was trying them all out. Finally, tentatively, the fingers tapped out, "Yes, I'll go."

I was about to get up, but the mind behind the fingers clearly had more to say.

"I've decided to publish," they wrote.

It took me a second or two to figure out what she had meant. Publish. Publicize. Tell the world of her discovery. This was news to me. I'd thought after 35 had seen the future, she had to understand how pointless this would be. Anyway, wasn't that what had already happened? "But Frank said you told him you'd destroy it before you'd let him mess up what you'd just fixed," I typed.

"I haven't said anything yet," my fingers slowly tapped out.

"You will," I wrote.

"No one tells me what to say."

My God, that sounded just like me when I was her age. I typed back, "I thought you understood that publishing the results might alter everything that happened afterwards."

"Worked very hard for this. Deserve credit for what I've discovered."

"But this is the most perfect outcome," I wrote. "You are respected, loved. Don't ruin this!"

"One small difference won't change much," was the reply.

I was livid. "THINK!" I wrote. "You mustn't change anything! You don't know yet about chaos theory. The butterfly effect—a small change at one time and place may result in large differences to a later state. A faint flutter of a butterfly in Mexico might bring on a tsunami in Japan. You publish and God knows what happens. I'll walk out of this lab into a world where Frank is dead and Caleb is the President of the United States!"

I was sure that I had convinced her then, because my fingers merely trembled, poised above the keyboard. A few moments went by before the fingers began to write.

"Haven't decided yet."

"But you never published," I typed furiously. "Even after you knew the machine worked, even after you returned from 2012. If you had published, Frank would have known it worked, but he didn't. You didn't do this."

"Have not done anything."

"But you have."

"Not yet. Free to decide."

Free to make mistakes, was what I thought. Free to burn bras and to be arrested and go to jail. Free to drive drunk and crash and burn. Free to be a young idiot and destroy your life.

"No!" I shouted as I typed. "You can't do this! I won't let you."

"G o i n g   t o   p u b l i s h .   F u c k   y o u ."

"Well," I wrote, with similar obstinacy, "I just won't send you back, then."

All of a sudden, I felt an intense tug from within my body, an irresistible force pulling me upright and lifting me off the chair onto my legs. I tried to grab onto the table, but some foreign force broke my hold and I was dragged backwards. All I had under my control was my mouth.

"You little shit," I shouted as I staggered, against my will, into the backroom. "You know nothing about life, always shooting your mouth off, always getting me into trouble. Here I just spent four months and great effort trying to undo one of your messes. Just so that I could secure your future! And all you want to do is get your god-damned credit. Believe me it won't buy happiness."

My fingers, without me, set the mechanism to 5:04 on May 3, 1987.

"DON'T YOU DARE PUBLISH!" I yelled. "YOU'LL RUIN EVERYTHING!"

Hands reached out to stuff the helmet on my head. I dropped heavily into the chair, unable to break the hold of the muscles forcing me down. My right hand shot up by itself and pressed the button.

This time there was not a whoosh but a suction; a sensation not of disembodiment, but of emptiness. She was gone. I exhaled, exhausted. I tried out my arms and legs; wiggled my fingers and toes. Everything worked. From the perspective of the lab, nothing seemed to have changed. So far, so good.

I locked the backroom and closed up the iPad, slipping it back into my briefcase. I took the elevator downstairs on my way to my eleven o'clock class. Despite the fact that my iPhone was trumpeting a barrage of new texts in the few minutes it took to go downstairs, not a thing seemed amiss until I heaved open the front doors of the building.

"Dr. Braverman!" some present-day version of Janie Carr in ripped jeans shouted, her iPhone pushed up into my face, clicking pictures of my open mouth. "What do you have to say about winning the Nobel Prize in physics?!"

"The Nobel!" I screamed. "I won the Nobel?!" My knees grew weak and my mind went blank. "Well," I said. "Well, I...."

In the background my iPhone was blaring with texts. "Congrats—Mark!" Beep! "Best regards!—Garriston Admin," Beep! "Knew it all along!—Edwin".

In an instant, a group of students had gathered around us, all yelling questions at me. "Did you know?" "Were you surprised?" "Are you going to Sweden?"

My phone was ringing. "Dr. Braverman?" it said when I put it to my ear. "It's Elliot Adams of the *Star-Ledger*. I understand they've awarded the physics Nobel to you alone. What's your reaction to all this?"

"To me alone?" I couldn't help asking. But what about

Frank? Without him, I could never have brought the project to completion. Wasn't he nominated, too?

"Yes," he replied. "Didn't you know? And that means the entire 1.1 million dollars is yours to do with whatever you choose. What do you plan to do with all that money?"

"1.1 million dollars!" I cried out. This was unbelievable! How long had I fantasized about this? I could set up a new lab. Do any number of experiments I'd all but dreamed of....It was all too much to think about, too much to process. I absolutely couldn't decide anything until I talked to Frank.

I returned to the man on the phone. "Sorry. Mr. Adams is it? At this point, I have simply no idea," I said and hit the end button.

Ring. "Dr. Braverman? This is Michelle Davenport of *The New York Times*. How do you feel about the honor of being one of only a few women to ever win a Nobel prize in physics?

"One of the few women!" I echoed happily.

In the company of Marie Curie! Forever in the history books!

...But, I suddenly wondered, how the hell did this even get out? Maybe Frank called the papers. After all, I told the two of them last night. But the Nobel! How could everything have happened in one night?

"A great honor, of course," I said and clicked off.

Ring. "Dr. Braverman. Harold Cohen of the *Philadelphia Inquirer*. Just wanted your reaction to finally being awarded the prize after a quarter of a century of waiting…"

A quarter of a century….Oh, no!

"Shock," I said, punching *end*.

The girl with the ripped jeans was back, her iPhone an inch away from my nose. "This must be quite a surprise. How do you feel about all this, Dr. Braverman?"

The sweet savor of triumph had begun to turn sour in my mouth. What did I feel? I felt sick. "No comment," I said and began to shove my way through the crowd, students trailing behind me.

The mob followed me to my car, where they gaped at me through the windshield as I pulled my iPhone, still tooting and honking, from my pocket and dialed Frank's cell number. But all it did was ring.

I got out, students still streaming behind me, and ran to Frank's old office. I was winded by the time I got there, but, thankfully, I had lost my entourage. I staggered to the door and was about to open it when I noticed the plaque on the door said, "Nina Mascallier."

"NO!" I yelled, running unsteadily out the building and back to my car. I unlocked the door with a trembling hand and got in. My watch said 11:15. To hell with my eleven o'clock class; I had to get home.

I drove like a maniac back to my little house, left the car in the driveway, galloped up the stairs and unlocked the front door. There, among the arched windows, plastered ceilings with their exposed wooden beams stood my old dented coffee table and the dusty ceramic *tchotchkas*.

Gone were the light-colored modular set, the glass table, the potted plant.

"Frank!" I shouted, frantically running from room to room. "Frank! Frank!" But the sound just echoed around the empty house.

About the Author

Bonnie Rozanski is the author of seven other novels, including Banana Kiss and Borderline (both published by Porcupine's Quill). Borderline was shortlisted for Foreword's Book of the Year and received a silver medal at the Independent Publishers' Book Awards. She currently lives with her husband in Philadelphia, but has resided in Hong Kong, Toronto, and all over the U.S. With degrees in Psychology and Artificial Intelligence, always fascinated by the human mind, Bonnie writes on matters touching on consciousness and the human condition.